Bear in Boots

Bearytales
Book 7

Sue Brown

*An explosive found family romance in the **Bearytales in the Wood** world.*

Brad feels out of place in his tight-knit family. His six gay Daddy brothers are all coupled up, leaving Brad as the lone Daddy without a boy to love. The drama of the past two years has eased and now, he's lonely.

Brad has always found solace in his barn, where he spends his days blowing things up and writing poetry about the explosive chaos. He's even gotten a publishing contract although he isn't sure what he's meant to do with it.

Then a shy young man turns up at Christmas Tree farm from his publisher. He's meant to be there to illustrate Brad's book, but what he can't remember is he and Brad have met before. The rest of the family can though, from the smirks.

No matter what he wants, Eric knows he's there just until the book is complete. Brad wants him to stay forever in his arms. It's an impossible choice for Eric. Then danger knocks at the cabin door...

"I wrote a book about seven brothers on the side of a mountain who saved one boy, and he changed the world."

Bradley Brenner

Chapter One

Brad

"**B**rad, are you in there?"

Brad held his breath and kept quiet, hoping Harry would go away.

"He's in there. He's got to be. The cabin rattled ten minutes ago," Gruff said.

Damn, Brad had forgotten about that. The explosion had been bigger than he'd anticipated.

"Maybe he's unconscious," Damien rumbled.

Brad rolled his eyes at his eldest brother's suggestion. Trust Damien to go straight to the worst-case scenario. Like Brad would knock himself out after the experience he had with explosions.

"What are you guys doing?" Aaron asked. "Why are you all huddled around the door?"

"It's lunchtime. Lyle is cooking dinner. He sent us to find Brad," Harry said.

"No, he sent me," Gruff pointed out. "You lot just came along for the ride...and to get out of helping my boy."

"True," Harry agreed. "It was getting tense in there."

"If you try and tell the prince of the potato peeler that he's doing it wrong, you deserve the ear-bashing you received," Aaron said bluntly. He was Jake's boy and never minced his words. After years of working in the Tin Bar and having to be polite to drunk Daddies, he went straight for the jugular. "What were you thinking?"

Brad nearly groaned out loud, clapping a hand over his mouth in case he gave himself away. Upsetting Vinny, the aforementioned prince of the potato peeler, was a really bad idea. He'd be sulking for days. Damien would be upset because his boy was sulking, and then none of them would be able to sit down and talk to Vinny about their day. It was a thing. All the family did it. Potato time was therapy time for whoever needed it. Brad had written poems about it.

"I didn't mean to upset him," Harry protested.

"Well, you have," Damien said. "It's going to take me the rest of the day to calm him down."

"Why aren't you with him?" Aaron said pointedly.

"He told me to go away," Damien muttered. "Me. His Daddy."

"He just wants to cry on Lyle's shoulder while no one else is there to see it. You can punish him later. Now hurry up and find your brother. My balls are ready to climb inside my body, it's so cold out here." For a boy surrounded by Daddies twice his size, he was free with the orders.

Inside the barn, Brad sighed. He didn't want to miss lunch, his belly rumbled just at the thought, but he didn't want to eat with his brothers and their boys.

It was hard for him now. He was lonely. How a man could be lonely in a family of thirteen men he didn't know. But Brad was. His six brothers had all found their boys and he was single. He'd told himself it didn't matter, he'd always been happy to be a lone wolf, but that was before he was faced with the reality of living with six loved-up couples.

Lately, he'd taken to hiding in his barns during the day rather than sharing the family meals, then spending his evenings in town at the Tin Bar and staying overnight at the motel. But that was lonely too and he wistfully remembered the times he and his brothers used to drink together in the bar and cause mayhem.

"Brad!" Damien bellowed.

"Careful, big man. You'll cause an avalanche," Aaron muttered. "Open the door."

"We don't do that," Harry said.

"Do what?"

"Open the door. In case he's about to blow something up. It could get messy."

This was an unspoken rule. No one interrupted Brad without warning. PJ had done it once and spent an entire summer waiting on his brother, hand and foot, as he recovered from his injuries.

"He knows we're here," Gruff pointed out. "We've been talking for long enough. He's hiding and hoping we'll go away."

Brad flinched. His baby brother was right, but he didn't have to say it out loud.

"Get out of the way."

Then the barn door was flung open. Brad stared at Aaron in the doorway, flanked by his three brothers towering over him. It looked like a Target advert for men's flannel shirts.

"It's lunchtime," Aaron snapped. "Are you done hiding?"

"I'm kinda busy," Brad lied. "I'll come in later."

Damien growled in exasperation. "It's a family meal. We always eat together."

They did. Brad knew this. And even Red, who struggled with the family idea, joined in. But—

Brad found himself herded out before he'd even completed the thought. Harry shut the barn door and they all headed to the big cabin.

Damien slung a meaty arm around Brad's shoulders. As the two eldest brothers they'd always been close. "You know hiding is a bad thing, right?"

He had hidden in the barns a lot when he was trying to avoid Vinny. His brothers had staged an intervention then, too.

"I didn't think anyone had noticed," Brad admitted, leaning into his older brother, just for a moment.

"We noticed," Harry said from behind him, and Gruff grunted.

"I know why you're hiding," Damien said, "and I'm sorry. It's gotta be hard for you. But I hate the thought you don't want to spend time with us."

Brad flinched. He knew his absence would be a sore point with Damien. Since the Kingdom orphanages had been closed and months had passed with the family at home, the clawing need to stay together had eased, but his big old sappy brother was always going to be the one to suffer if one of the family was away for too long.

"I'll try and spend more time with you," he muttered.

Damien hugged him closer. "Thanks."

Brad didn't need to look at him to know he was choked up. Sap.

The warmth of the kitchen was a relief. Rexy, Vinny's dog, was in his usual spot by the stove when Lyle cooked.

Close enough to get any treats that could be dropped but not enough to get under Lyle's feet.

Vinny flung himself at Damien who scooped him up and took him out of the kitchen.

"Don't take too long to kiss and make up," Lyle yelled after them.

Brad sniffed. Whatever was in the oven smelled fabulous. "Meatloaf?"

Lyle smiled at him. "It's your favorite."

"You made this for me?"

"I did. And mashed potatoes and greens."

Brad swallowed hard. He was choked up at the thought Lyle had made a meal especially for him. "Thanks, Lyle."

He received a sweet smile in return. "You're welcome. Now wash up and sit at the table."

Lyle was his youngest brother Gruff's boy and without a doubt, the best cook in the family. Vinny was a close second, and despite his grumbles, Jack was learning too. It didn't mean to say the brothers couldn't cook. It just meant Lyle did it better. Brad thought Lyle was even better than his mom, but she wouldn't have minded.

One by one all the brothers came in until the huge pine table was full and everyone was laughing and joking. Brad pasted a huge smile on his face and joined in. He would fake happiness if it was the last thing he did. He owed his family that.

They were about to eat when someone knocked at the kitchen door.

"Are we expecting anyone?" Gruff asked, but everyone shook their heads.

Being so far up the mountain, they usually knew who was visiting. Recently, the unknown visitors had been unwelcome, to say the least, so they let it be known that people had to message before dropping in.

"Someone answer the door before the food gets cold," PJ grumbled.

Gruff stood and Jack nudged his Daddy.

"You go too."

PJ grumbled again but he obediently followed Gruff over to the door because he'd do anything for Jack, and Damien joined them.

"You don't have to scare the living daylights out of them," Lyle murmured.

"Until we know if they're friend or foe we do," Brad said.

Gruff opened the door. "Can I help you? Hey, don't I know you?"

"Uh...I don't think so." A man sounded confused.

"Okay," Gruff said. "Can I help you then?'

"I...uh...is Bradley Brenner at home?"

It took a moment for Brad to realize they were asking for him. No one had called him by his full name in years.

"Uh..." Gruff sounded as bemused as he was. He looked over his shoulder. "Brad?"

"Who is it?" Brad asked.

A man peered around the man-mountains in his way. Brad's first impression was of a young man and tall if he hadn't been standing next to PJ, sweet-faced, with light brown hair and huge gray eyes blinking behind large, rimmed glasses. "Mr. Brenner?"

Brad got to his feet. "I'm Brad Brenner. I'm sorry, who are you?"

He waved at his brothers to get out of the way. They shuffled back to their seats, leaving the stranger, dressed in a jacket and jeans more suitable to warmer climates than

Kingdom Mountain in the dead of winter, shivering in the doorway.

Brad blinked. "Eric, is that you?"

The man stared at him blankly. "Uh...yes. How did you know my name?"

Eric

Being confronted with three men scowling at him was disconcerting, especially the two huge guys blocking the doorway. Then another ten men stared at him from a table piled high with food.

Eric's stomach growled at the delicious aroma. Was that meatloaf? He tried to sniff without being obvious. His mouth watered. It was meatloaf, one of Eric's all-time favorite meals.

But he was here to do a job, not fill his belly. He was cold and hungry. It had been a long ride here. And now his client, who was another man mountain, had no idea he was coming. Eric just prayed they didn't throw him out. He wasn't sure he could face that road so soon. He swore he'd driven up with his eyes shut.

The biggest one squinted at him. "Isn't he that guy you stuck your...ow!"

The other bear had just elbowed him in the ribs. "What did you do that for?"

"Just bring him over here," a young guy, maybe Eric's age, said. "He looks frozen. Join us for lunch, Eric. There's a space next to Brad."

Eric turned to Brad, who still stared at him, looking just as confused as he was. "Is that okay?" he asked hesitantly.

Brad seemed to shake himself. "Sure. Come meet my family."

Eric was sure he mumbled "...again," but he must have misheard.

This was how Eric found himself between Brad and a much smaller blond-haired boy...man, Eric corrected himself hastily.

"Eric, it's good to see you again," the small man said.

Eric frowned. "Do I know you?"

There was a silence around the table and Eric caught them looking at each other.

"You don't remember me...us?" Brad asked.

Eric bit his lip. "I have amnesia. I was in a car accident last year. I don't remember anything before then."

They all looked horrified. Eric was used to that expression. What he wasn't used to was people who said they knew him.

"The food is getting cold," one of the big men grumbled. He wasn't big, he was massive, and all muscle. No wonder he liked his food.

"Quick introductions," the little guy said, "then you can eat. I'm Vinny. This is Damien. He's mine." He pointed to one of the men with a graying beard who had greeted him at the door. "And so is Rexy."

Eric blinked. The little man had two boyfriends?

"Rexy's my dog," Vinny said, pointing to a small black mutt of indeterminate breed, sacked out in front of the stove.

"Oh." Eric nodded to show Vinny he understood.

What had he just walked into?

"Down, boy," the man said, with a fond smile. "He's Brad's."

Eric's jaw dropped and then he heard a choking sound on the other side of him. He turned to see Brad staring across him.

"What the hell, Damien?" Brad's voice cracked.

"I'm sorry, Eric," the man who'd invited him to sit said. "You'll get used to us. It's always like this. I'm Lyle. This is my...boyfriend. This is Gruff."

He pointed to a huge man on one side of him. Gruff looked younger than Brad or Vinny's guy. He also looked unhappy at something Lyle had said.

"Not again."

Eric turned to see who had spoken. Massive guy smiled at him but there was a cautious edge Eric didn't understand.

"Eric, I'm PJ. This is my boy, Jack."

Jack waved at him. He looked to be in his mid-twenties. His smile was friendly enough.

"Look, kid, we're all gay," PJ said. "Do you have a problem with that?"

"No," Eric squeaked.

"Good. We're all brothers. The big dudes are my brothers by blood. The little dudes are my brothers by love. No, Damien, you can't start sniffling now." PJ turned to fix his gaze on Eric. "And we're all in Daddy/boy relationships. Do you have a problem with that, too?"

"Way to go, PJ," one of the younger guys said. "The poor kid's just walked through the door and—"

"I'm not walking on eggshells again," PJ declared. "We did that before, and it hurt all of us. Red dealt with us and so can—"

"Red had time to process," Brad interrupted, scowling at PJ.

"No, I don't have a problem." Eric blushed as all eyes turned on him. "I don't know much about...that..."

"You did," PJ muttered.

"Shut up, Daddy," Jack snapped. "Let Eric talk." He smiled at Eric. "Sorry, my Daddy doesn't mean to be rude."

Eric nodded. "I don't have a problem with who or what you are. I'm just here to draw pictures," he got out in a rush.

"Thank heaven for that," Lyle said. "Now let's eat. Help yourself, Eric."

But Brad took the plate Lyle offered and heaped it full of meatloaf and mashed potatoes and greens.

"Is that just for me?" Eric asked faintly.

Lyle chuckled. "There's one rule in this house. Eat what you can. No one will force you to eat."

Thank goodness for that. Eric would be there for days if he had to finish the whole plate.

"Do you know about us?" Brad said, his voice low as everyone started eating and chatting.

"Some." Eric pitched his voice low although he wasn't sure Brad could hear him above the noise around the table. "Not much."

His publisher, David Petersen, had been reticent about what he'd told Eric. Just that it was urgent. He should have been warned about the family. Not that he minded, but it could have been a thing.

It was a thing. They knew who he was! And he still didn't.

"Some of the boys have issues around food because of how they were brought up. Lyle, Vinny, and Red all struggle to eat and some of the boys who visit us are the same. I'm telling you this because we don't make a big deal of it here."

"I have food issues, but I don't know if that's since the accident."

Eric wasn't sure why he needed to tell Brad something so personal, but Brad just nodded as if he understood.

"No one is starved or beaten," Brad continued. "We take care of our boys."

Eric stared at him. "What?"

Brad shook his head. "Dammit, they shouldn't have sent you in blind."

"It wasn't meant to be me," Eric admitted. "I was called in at the last moment because your illustrator had a bereavement. I'm new to the company." The look Brad cast him didn't reassure him. Eric licked his lips. "I'm new, but I know what I'm doing. I can show you." He went to find his bag, but Brad placed his hand over his. For some reason, his touch was very comforting.

"Eat. Or Lyle will get upset."

Eric took a mouthful of the meatloaf and nearly moaned. It was divine.

"Good, huh?"

"More than good." Eric shoveled half the plate before he came up for air. It had been months since he'd eaten like this. Money had been tight, and it had taken him a long while to find a publisher willing to take a chance on him.

No one seemed to notice or care, and Eric continued eating as they all chatted.

"Who is your boy?" Eric asked, looking around the table. There seemed to be one missing.

"Big brother is young, free, and single," PJ said with a smirk. "If you're asking. Just like he was before."

"Before?" Eric asked, confused.

PJ raised a bushy eyebrow. "You really don't remember you and big brother here—"

Eric stared at him. "What?"

"Shut the fuck up, PJ. Sorry, Lyle. Leave Eric alone, yeah?" Brad dug into his pocket and stuck a note in a jar on the table. "This is our swear jar. It doesn't stop us from cursing, but we get a good Thanksgiving dinner from it. Also, PJ is a wind-up merchant."

"So I noticed." Eric swallowed. "I'm sorry, I didn't mean to touch a nerve."

Brad sighed. "You didn't. He did." He jabbed a finger at his brother. "He's just being crass and unsubtle."

But Eric wasn't blind. It was one of his skills as an illustrator. He could see this was a touchy subject. It had to be hard for Brad when the rest of his family were all in relationships.

"Anyway, that's not what you're here for." Brad frowned. "I mean, what are you here for?"

"I'm illustrating your book. Didn't they tell you? I'm here to get ideas from you, talk about the poems and what they mean."

"Have you read his poems?" A redhead with a huge rusty bushy beard said, wearing a smirk. Brad scowled but the other guy didn't notice or didn't care.

Eric nodded. "They're beautiful and very profound."

The guy's mouth fell open. At least, Eric thought it did. He wasn't so sure under the beard and mustache. "You understand them?"

Eric furrowed his brow, hoping he wasn't about to make a fool of himself. "I read them as comparing the phases of an explosion to the transient state of our emotions."

The table went quiet. He'd been about to say more but everyone was staring at him. "But I could be wrong."

"You're not," Brad rumbled, a huge smile from ear to ear flashing pearly-white teeth at him. "At least they didn't send me a total philistine."

Eric held back a flinch. He knew who they'd been planning to send. Brad was lucky. The elderly illustrator would have taken one look at the table of men and bolted. Maybe that's why he'd been chosen in Tomas's place rather than one of the experienced staff and the bereavement was just an excuse.

"I read all your poems. I have ideas sketched out already. I emailed them to you but you didn't reply, so they sent me up here."

Because the publisher was starting to tear his hair out at their client's lack of communication. Eric was on a mission. David Peterson had been insistent.

"Get this book finished or you're both done."

He was starting to understand what the problem was.

"Looks like you're gonna have to quit hiding, big brother," one of the other big men drawled. He was cuddling a younger guy with dark hair and a haunted expression pressed up against him. "Ignore anything he says, Eric."

Eric gave him an uncertain smile. "Mr. Brenner is my client. I want him to be happy."

Before anyone could respond, Brad got to his feet, his chair tipped over, clattering to the floor.

"If anyone replies to that, we're gonna have words. Understand?"

Eric stared wide-eyed at the growl in his voice. "Mr. Brenner?"

Brad looked down at him. "Call me Brad. There are too many Mr. Brenners here. They'll all say yes. Let's go talk, Eric."

"Brad—" Lyle started.

Brad's expression softened. He was clearly fond of the young man. "Yeah?"

"Show Eric our old room. He can use that to sleep in."

"Not the small one?" Brad asked.

"No point with all the other rooms free."

"It's okay," Eric hastened to say. "I've got a room in the motel in town."

"You stay with us," Brad insisted. "You're not driving the mountain road in the dark. Besides, the food and the bed are better here. We'll go down tomorrow and get your gear."

"Are you sure?" Eric asked, uncertain but so relieved he didn't have to face that road again that day.

"It always starts like this," Lyle assured him.

Eric wrinkled his brow. "What starts?"

Brad looked down at him. "I want you to ignore what any of them say, okay?"

"Okay," Eric said, anxious not to upset his client.

"See, he's taking orders already."

Eric didn't know which brother muttered that but from the yelp and scowl, it was PJ again, and Jack had just elbowed him in the ribs.

Maybe Eric should call his publisher. He'd heard about Brad and his family, but he was totally out of his depth with seven gay Daddy bears and their six boys. He pushed aside the thought of how handsome these guys were, especially the hot, single one next to him. He was here on business for the publisher. All he had to do was get the book finished. He could do that, couldn't he?

Chapter Two

Brad

Two hours later, Brad stood outside the cabin, shivering a little in the cold night air despite the layers of clothing he wore. He needed the chill mountain air to clear his head. Eric had asked for some time to get himself sorted before they talked, and to be honest, Brad was glad of the time to decompress. He was back. Brad couldn't quite believe it. The boy who had haunted his dreams (and his fantasies) for months. And his boy couldn't remember their previous encounter.

He had to admit he was kind of offended by that. Was he that forgettable? Brad hadn't forgotten a moment of their one night together. He'd had his fair share of men and boys, until he realized he wasn't getting anything from these encounters. That's when Brad retreated to his barn and started blowing shit up. Between the farm, his chemistry experimentations, and his poetry, Brad didn't have a lot of free time, but he'd never forgotten the one night with Eric.

He'd always hoped that Eric would get in contact with him again, but when he didn't, he assumed that the boy had wanted to leave his old life behind him. It had been a little galling to Brad to be so easily left behind, but he knew Eric needed a fresh start.

Brad stared up at the cloudless sky. It was a clear night and the stars shone brightly on the crisp snow. There was a new moon, a crescent barely visible in the night sky.

Time for a fresh start. But would that be with or without Eric?

"Brad?"

"Hey." Brad turned at the soft and uncertain question. Eric stood there, shivering, in a thin sweater and jeans and socks.

"I didn't know if you'd be in your cabin."

"I...uh...haven't moved in there yet," Brad admitted.

Because he didn't want to be all alone. He'd never been alone in his life.

"You're going to freeze," he said roughly.

"I just wanted to talk to you. I'm not cold." Eric's teeth chattered making a liar out of him, like Brad didn't know he was cold to his bones.

"Come with me. I'm not letting you get pneumonia. And you know this mountain. You should know better."

Eric furrowed his brow and Brad sighed. Did the boy even remember he grew up on the mountain at all? Brad herded Eric inside as if he was a recalcitrant sheep, went to the coat rack in the hall and grabbed one of the jackets.

"Put your shoes on." The shoes weren't suitable, but they'd do for now. He waited until Eric had stamped his feet into the shoes and handed him the jacket. "I know this is going to swallow you whole, but at least you'll stay warm."

He helped Eric put on the jacket which came down to Eric's knees.

"I look like I'm dressing up in my father's clothes," Eric grumbled, his expression disgusted.

"Tomorrow we'll go into the attic and find you clothes that will fit." Brad saw Eric's skeptical expression and he chuckled. "We have an attic full of all our clothes we outgrew. Our mom kept them all. She was a bit of a hoarder. All the boys who come into the house wear them. It's a thing."

Eric regarded him for one moment. "What makes you think I'm a boy?"

"Aren't you?" Brad challenged.

"I don't know," Eric admitted. "I don't know anything." He tapped his head. "In there is empty. I don't know anything about anything."

"You may not remember your life before your accident, but I imagine what you are is inside you. It doesn't go away. It's innate and hard to forget." Brad couldn't imagine ever forgetting he was gay and a Daddy. It was who he was, the whole of him. He thought it was probably the same for his brothers.

"Do you know if you're gay?"

Eric nodded. "I knew that as soon as I woke up and the hot doctor was leaning over me. I told him he looked like a movie star. I can't even remember which one."

Brad laughed. "See, that's inside you. I think being a boy is the same."

"Do you think that's why David sent me here? Because he knew I'd understand you?"

"How would he know? I thought you said the illustrator had a bereavement."

Eric blushed. "That's what they told me to tell you. I don't know if it's true."

Brad knew what outsiders thought of them. His family had taken hostility from some of the town folk all their lives. It was water off a duck's back. He was more interested in Eric's return than anything else. "Maybe the other guy really didn't want to come here and David just needed someone else."

"Maybe," Eric said, his eyes wide and uncertain.

Brad handed him a hat and gloves. "Let's go outside for a moment, boy."

Back on the verandah, they stood in silence for a few minutes, staring up at the stars. But this time, Brad was hyper-alert to the man standing next to him. He turned to looked at Eric when he sighed.

"It's beautiful here. I feel like I know it so well, like I've been here before."

Brad regarded him for a moment. "You really don't remember, do you?"

Eric gave a slightly bitter laugh. "I keep telling you I don't. My memory exists from the time I woke up in the hospital, and even that is fuzzy. I don't know if I have any family or friends. I know nothing about myself, except I can draw."

"How did you discover that?" Brad asked curiously.

"I was made to do art therapy in the hospital as part of my recovery process. It was natural, like breathing."

"So what happened after that?"

"Eventually, I left the hospital. They needed the bed. I had to find somewhere to live and a job. From the paper-work they found on me I was supposed to start an art degree, but I missed the start of the semester and my brain was too fuzzy to study. The college agreed to hold my place for a year." Eric grimaced. "I've been doing any job I could find and applying to anywhere I could draw. There's not much call for my line of work, but I met David Peterson by chance and begged him for an opportunity. And here I am."

Brad looked at the boy swamped in his huge jacket and took one of his hands. "Eric, I know you're not going to believe this, but you've turned up at the one place in the world with people who know who you are and can fill in some of the blanks for you."

He heard Eric catch his breath and felt a shiver run through him, but this time it wasn't from the cold.

"Don't play with me," Eric begged.

"I'm not. I know this is hard to believe, but as I keep telling you, you've been here before."

"I have?"

"In fact, you grew up on this mountain, just up the mountain road."

"I did?" Eric's eyes were huge.

Brad smiled at him. "You did. Vinny, Lyle, and Matt all grew up with you."

"You mean...?"

Brad nodded. "You were a Kingdom boy, just like they were."

Eric's knees buckled, and Brad put his arms around him, and swept him into his arms, just in time to save him from collapsing to the decking.

He held Eric against him and caressed his hair. "I know it's hard to believe, and I didn't intend to dump all this information on you in one go."

"It's just hard to process, you know?" Eric confessed, his voice shaky.

"You're not the first boy to find his way here and I think that we are put here for this reason. All of our boys have had trauma in their lives. Not all of them are Kingdom boys, but they've suffered in one way or another."

"But I haven't suffered." Eric said. "At least, I don't remember it. I don't remember anything."

"Maybe that's a good thing," Brad said quietly.

Eric sniffled, and took a step back, leaving Brad's arms, feeling empty. "There's something else, isn't there? Your brothers knew me too, and you greeted me by name."

"We do."

"But how?"

"You have been here before. Your subconscious is right. Lyle had a birthday party a year ago and you were here. Vinny invited all the Kingdom boys who knew Lyle. I met you then."

"You did?"

Brad gave him a wry smile. "You were leaving to start your course. It was your way off the mountain. I drove you down to get the bus. You must've had the accident soon after."

Eric nodded slowly. "I don't remember being on a bus. But I was on my way to college when it happened. I was hitchhiking. Maybe I wanted to save money. I was hit by a truck. The driver wasn't paying attention to the road. I was lucky to live."

Brad thought about all the times he imagined Eric living his best life at college. Having fun, screwing all the boys. Never thinking for one moment his boy was in hospital fighting for his life.

"Didn't you have any paperwork on you?"

Eric was a Kingdom boy. They all had paperwork

which should've come back to Lyle. He knew Lyle had made sure he had it.

Eric grimaced. "The police said the trucker probably took everything he could off me so that I wouldn't be identified. The college paperwork was tucked away and he missed it."

Brad stared at him in horror. "You were a victim of a hit-and-run?"

"I was lucky, someone found me soon afterward, and I ended up in hospital nearby. The combination of how soon I was found, and how close the hospital was, was the only thing that saved my life."

Brad couldn't help himself. He swept Eric into his arms and held him, so close, his cheek resting on Eric's head as his tears dripped into Eric's soft hair. He would never have known, but for this one fated chance that a publisher would send an unknown artist to a rural mountain to illustrate an unknown poet's work. It was like the fates had put them together again. Brad was not a believer in any faith, but he had an understanding that each person had a purpose on this earth. Since the moment Lyle walked into his family's life, their purpose had been explained. Now it was his turn to help someone.

"All you have to do is put a little trust in me," he murmured into Eric's hair.

"I do trust you," Eric said, his voice muffled into Brad's neck. "I don't know why, but I realized I trusted you from the first moment I saw you."

Brad took a deep breath. There was something else he needed to tell Eric before he could relax. He wasn't the type of guy to keep secrets. "I'm going to tell you this because I don't want it slipping out from anyone else. PJ has a big mouth and he won't be able to keep it quiet."

Eric raised his head, and Brad gazed down into his eyes, smiling slightly at his askew glasses. "He made a comment, didn't he, when I first arrived."

Brad nodded. "At the party... You and I... We...uh..." Was he ever going to be able to spit this out? "We... uh...got together."

"Got together?"

"We hooked up."

Brad saw Eric's eyes go comically wide, and his mouth dropped open.

"You and me?" Eric gasped.

Brad wasn't sure how to take that. Was he really that repulsive? "Just the once."

Eric

"Oh wow." Eric managed. "That's...not what I was expecting when I turned up here today."

Brad took a step back, putting distance between them. "It was consensual. You can ask my family."

Eric realized Brad thought he was horrified by the idea. "No, I didn't mean..." He took Brad's hand. "I was just surprised, is all."

Brad regarded him for a long moment. "You don't think I took advantage of you?"

"I can't remember anything about it," Eric confessed. "But you don't seem like the type of man who would take advantage of anyone...unless they wanted it." He smirked and to his relief, saw an answering quirk in the corner of Brad's mouth. "I'm assuming I did want it."

"Oh yeah," Brad said, his voice all smoky and raw. "You wanted it."

"Thank God," Eric said relieved. "I can't think why I'd have turned down an invitation from a sexy man like you."

Brad snorted. "You leaped on me, my boy. By the woodpile."

"I did?" Eric could never imagine being that bold, but then he couldn't remember the man he'd been before.

"You did," Brad assured him with a full-on smirk now. "And I'm getting over my butt hurt. I've never been that forgettable." But this time he was teasing and Eric breathed easier. The last thing he wanted to do was upset this wonderful Daddy Bear.

"I wish I could remember," he said wistfully.

Brad stepped forward into Eric's space. "May I kiss you?"

Eric nodded and waited. Brad tilted his chin and bent to kiss him. Eric closed his eyes and sank into the kiss. It was soft, gentle, prickly with his mustache and beard, but so tender Eric felt stinging in the back of his eyes. Brad wrapped his arms around him and held him tight.

"Take it inside," someone grumbled. "It's too cold to make out here and you're blocking the door."

Eric blushed as Brad raised his head. Alec and Matt wore twin smirks from the bottom of the stoop.

"There are other doors," Brad said pointedly.

"Then we couldn't make fun of you, big brother," Alec teased as he and Matt jogged past him hand-in-hand. Matt mouthed an apology at Eric, then they disappeared inside.

"They have a point," Brad agreed. "It's very cold out here."

He guided Eric into the kitchen. The warmth hit Eric like a wave and he yawned.

"Sorry. It's been a long day."

Brad took him into the hall and stripped him of his outer layers, then he steered him to the stairs.

"It's too early to go to bed," Eric almost whined. In truth, he had no idea what the actual time was. "I should start work."

"It's nearly nine o'clock. Get an early night and catch up on your sleep."

It was an order, if a gentle one. And Eric realized he'd been following Brad's orders since he arrived. Was that what it was like having a Daddy? Handing over those decisions to him? Eric wasn't sure how he felt about that.

But at the door of the bedroom, Brad left him there with a gentle kiss on the forehead and told him to sleep well. "Don't rush up tomorrow. I've got chores to do on the farm. Once they're done I'll have time to sit with you."

Eric nodded and vanished into the bedroom. He flopped down on the king size bed and stared out at the moonlight. That was the last he remembered.

* * *

Eric woke slowly, blinking as he took in the large bedroom. Brad had told him the room had been Gruff and Lyle's until they moved into the master bedroom when Damien and Vinny moved to their cabin. Now it was his for as long as he wanted it. He felt guilty intruding on the family, although not paying motel bills would please his publisher. They were a small family press and didn't have much money to spend on their employees.

He spotted a pile of clothes on the dresser that hadn't been there the previous night. He rolled out of bed and stretched, yawning, then scratching his belly.

Eric picked up the note on top of the clothes.

. . .

Hope these fit. There are plenty more to try.

B

Eric stroked his fingertip over the strong handwriting. He studied the jeans, t-shirts, and flannel shirts. They were well-worn but usable. Certainly warmer than what he had to wear. But what about underwear? Then he spotted his shabby backpack at the foot of the dresser. Someone had driven down to the motel and back this morning. He checked his phone. It was eight o'clock. What time did they get up?

He showered, shaved, and dressed in a red flannel shirt and faded jeans. They were a little large but not impossible, although he was self-conscious dressed in Brad's clothes. It wasn't as if they were any different to what anyone else was wearing. But maybe that was the point. It made him fit, part of the family, and he wasn't.

Eric wandered into the kitchen and found Vinny at the table, peeling potatoes. Rexy was asleep in front of the wood stove, on his back, paws in the air. He had a heart of white fur on his chest.

Vinny looked up and smiled at him. "Hi, are you looking for Brad?"

"Yes, I should start work soon," Eric admitted. "I'm not sure what I'm doing at the moment." He hesitated. "Brad says you know me from...before."

Vinny nodded. "I do. Matt knows you better because you helped him with the horses, but I remember you."

"Could you tell me about then?"

"Sure." Vinny glanced over at the stove. "Do you want a

hot chocolate? Lyle makes it. It's the best. We can drink that and you can help me peel potatoes."

Eric was aware of an edge in Vinny's tone he didn't understand, but he knew he was suddenly treading in dangerous waters. Was it always going to be like this?

"Tell me where the cups are, and I'll pour the chocolate," he suggested.

Vinny pointed to a cabinet above the stove. "Mine's the cup with the duckling. Use one of the stripy blue cups. They're for anyone's use."

"Which one is Brad's?" Eric asked as he pulled down two mugs.

"The one that says, 'Like cooking, only with explosions." Vinny chuckled. "Brad's cups don't last very long. They usually get broken in his experiments."

"I can imagine that."

Eric peered into the pan to discover it full of hot chocolate. He inhaled the aroma appreciatively. It smelled amazing. He found a ladle in a drawer and poured two cups. Then brought them to the table.

Vinny sighed happily as he wrapped his hands around his cup. Eric could have sworn he stroked the duckling first.

"Do you have another potato peeler?" Eric asked.

Vinny produced another as if by magic.

"You have a lot of helpers?"

"A few," Vinny agreed. "The family come and talk to me."

Eric took a potato and started to peel it. They worked in silence for several minutes, Eric at a much slower rate than Vinny.

"Why do you peel all the potatoes?" Eric asked.

"Because the family need potato time."

"I don't understand."

Vinny smiled at him. "You will."

Eric stared down at the potato in his hand. "What can't I remember?"

Vinny snorted. "I think the question is, what *can* you remember?"

"Nothing much," Eric confessed. "It's like I didn't exist before I woke up in hospital last year."

Vinny's expression was sympathetic. "That must be hard on you."

Eric stared at him. "Am I lucky to have forgotten the theme park?"

"Some," Vinny agreed. "It wasn't a good place."

"Were we abused?"

"I was, but I was always pushing and pushing. I hated the Greencoats and refused to obey their rules. Lyle was better behaved than I was. He just wanted a quiet life."

"And me?" Eric asked.

"I can't remember much about you," Vinny confessed. "I saw you in the tower once or twice. You said you'd disobeyed a Greencoat. That wasn't long before we were rescued."

"The tower?"

Vinny shuddered. "We were tortured there."

Eric licked his lips. He didn't want to ask questions, he didn't want to know about torture and pain, but it was part of his childhood. "I read about the Greencoats."

Vinny's expression darkened. "They were evil men."

"I wonder how many boys were disappeared. Would it have happened to us?"

Discovering he was a Kingdom boy brought its own terrors. How close had he been to being disappeared?

Then Vinny leaned forward and touched his wrist, bringing him back to the present. His expression was kind.

"It's all right, Eric. We survived. Just remember that. My Daddy saved me. You and I were saved by the Brenners and Lyle. Now Brad will take care of you."

Eric stared at him, then shook his head. "You don't understand. I'm only here to illustrate Brad's book."

Vinny shook his head. "You're here like all the boys in the house. Because you belong here. Aren't you?"

Chapter Three

Brad

The kitchen door slammed in Brad's face as he jogged up the stoop.

"Okay then," he muttered.

Someone was having a moment. He opened the door to find Red glaring at Harry.

"It's not my fault."

Brad edged around the two of them. If they were going to have a fight, he didn't want to be involved. Red was always loud when he was angry, his temper as fiery as his hair. He was still adjusting to life on the mountain. If Harry wasn't here, he would have left a long time ago, but he adored his Daddy and would do anything for him.

Harry crossed his arms, his face set in a fierce scowl. "Thunder could have been hurt."

That explained Harry's expression. He would never let anything bad happen to the horses. Alec had once let an abscess fester in his horse's hoof. She was only saved thanks to Harry's devotion and he didn't speak to Alec for weeks.

No one sat at the kitchen table and the potatoes were only half-done. They'd obviously fled.

Brad headed into the hall as new shouting erupted behind him. He found Eric and Vinny sitting on the stairs, the dog resting his head on Eric's knee. Eric caressed his head and the dog closed his eyes in ecstasy. Brad noted Eric wore the clothes he left on the dresser.

"Are you guys hiding?" He smirked at them.

"It was getting noisy," Vinny said.

"What happened?"

"Red left Thunder's stall open. He almost made it to the road. It was just lucky Damien found him."

Brad grimaced. Thunder was the last horse they needed on the loose. Damien's huge stallion, his temper was as legendary as his owner's. Damien and Harry adored him, Brad was wary but fond of him, everyone else kept their distance. Vinny was utterly petrified of him.

Brad raised an eyebrow. "I'm surprised Damien isn't shouting."

"He was. Harry told him to back off and he would deal with his boy."

"Why are we all sitting here?" Matt asked as he came down the stairs.

"It wasn't my fault," Red bellowed from the kitchen. "You were the last one in his stall."

"I told you to..."

The noise suddenly faded as a door slammed. They had obviously retreated outside.

"Ah." Matt nodded. "At least we can go back in the kitchen. We've run out of coffee in the office."

"Give it a minute," Brad suggested. "What were you doing up there?"

"I left Kingdom documents in Alec's old bedroom last

30

night. I didn't want them in our new home. I meant to take them to the office."

They waited but Red and Harry didn't come back in so they went into the kitchen. Matt to the coffee maker, and Vinny and Eric to the table.

Brad sat down next to Eric and smiled at him. "Are you okay? I'm sorry about the drama." He waved at the door.

Eric grinned. "It's okay. Vinny says it happens."

Brad very carefully said nothing as Vinny was notorious for yelling if he got upset. He heard Vinny's snort and looked up to see the boy grinning at him. He grinned back. He loved Damien's highly-strung and temperamental boy.

"We all bellow from time to time," he agreed.

"You guys tend to go hide," Vinny said.

Brad thought about it for a moment. "You have a point. Mom used to send us off in different directions and I guess we still do that. We're big guys. If we fight, we break things. Look at PJ." He raised his voice as his huge younger brother walked in, his boy behind him.

PJ scowled at him. "I haven't broken anything for a while."

Eric laughed and shook his head. "You're all as bad as each other."

"True," Brad agreed.

Eric suddenly remembered something. "Who brought my pack up? It was so early."

"I did," Matt said. "I had to go into town for supplies."

"Thanks," Eric said gratefully. "I'll give you the money for the check."

Matt waved his hand. "It's all settled."

"But—"

"Talk to your Daddy."

He poured four cups of coffee, stacked a tray with the

coffee and creamer pods and left the kitchen, leaving behind silence. Eric sucked in a breath.

Brad turned to Eric. "So my brothers, by blood and by love, never think about what they're saying. Just ignore them."

"Don't know what there is to ignore," PJ grumbled as he poured a hot chocolate for himself and Jack. "It's obvious he's the right boy for you. He understands your poems. None of the rest of us do."

Then they were gone and it left Eric and Brad and Vinny trying to avoid each other's gaze.

"I'm not going anywhere," Vinny snapped. "I've got the potatoes to peel."

"I should help," Eric said vaguely.

Brad stood and held out his hand to Eric. "No, you should come to my barn. Vinny, I promise to help you for the next week if you don't mind me taking Eric now."

Vinny grinned at him. "I'll hold you to that."

And Vinny would.

As Brad and Eric wandered to the barns, travel mugs filled with hot chocolate, Brad pointed out the cabins his brothers had moved into. They were all subtly different in shape and size.

"But not you," Eric said.

"Not yet. That's mine, over there." He pointed to one near the barns.

"Because it would be lonely?"

Brad gave him a tight smile. "I've been tumbling over people my entire life."

"They haven't gone far," Eric assured him.

"Far enough."

The silence stretched out uncomfortably. Brad cursed himself for being truthful.

"How did you get involved in amateur chemistry?" Eric asked suddenly.

Brad tried not to be offended at his description. After the years he'd been working, he was anything but amateur. "There was no money for college, but we did have a huge number of barns and a lot of space. So as long as I worked on the farm, my folks let me blow things up."

"Isn't it dangerous?"

"Not if you know what you're doing. I'm careful and I follow the rules."

"How do you get the chemicals? Don't you get into trouble with the authorities? Do they think you're making drugs or explosive for terrorists?"

Brad hesitated. "If I tell you a secret, do you promise not to tell my family, especially Damien?"

Eric raised an eyebrow. "I thought you didn't like secrets and lies."

"I don't. But this is the kind of secret where they'd just laugh at me and I'd never live it down."

"Go on then."

Brad opened the door to his barn. "This is the barn everyone sees me working in."

Eric peered in curiously. Brad saw it through his eyes. Homemade work tables filled with flasks, sinks at one end, a fume hood. Fire extinguishers and first aid kits lined one wall.

"Where are your chemicals?" Eric asked.

"They're locked up."

"So what's your secret?"

Brad led Eric to a door, unlocked it, and led him into his laboratory. "This is where I really work."

Eric's jaw dropped. "But this is the real deal."

Brad surveyed his small but fully equipped lab. "It is.

These days this is where I do most of my work. I work for the authorities. I have a small contract to...well, it doesn't matter what I do, but it's legit."

"You can't tell me?"

Brad shook his head.

"And none of your family know?"

"Harry and PJ do. They work on the farm too and taking on the contract meant I was going to have less time to help them. They agreed because the federal money helps us. Also if something goes wrong, they're trained to deal with fire and injuries."

Eric gazed around. "You still blow shit up."

"I do. The Feds were gonna shut me down. You're right. They don't like amateurs playing with chemicals, especially in our current climate. It used to be a lot more fun," Brad said almost wistfully. "This was the only way I could continue my research. And I only agreed to do that if I could stay working on the farm. It's a tiny lab beneath the radar. Most people don't know I exist."

"How do they let you do this?" Eric sounded awed.

"I'm really, really good at what I do."

"You should train someone to help you."

"That's the next step," Brad admitted. "I can't keep up the pace I'm at now. I don't have time for my poetry. It's why you never got a reply. But it's hard to find anyone who wants to work up here. I've told them I'm taking a break for a few weeks to finish our book."

From the smile on Eric's face, calling it our book had just made him very happy.

Eric shook his head. "You amaze me. Poet and scientist." He suddenly stepped into Brad's space and kissed his cheek.

Brad touched the spot where his lips had been, his insides all gooey.

And Daddy.

Hopefully. One day.

Eric

They walked back toward the cabin, ice crisping under their boots. Brad talked something about a job he'd had to do for someone called Josh Cooper. Eric wasn't really listening but he smiled and nodded every time Brad looked at him. He had other things to think about. Brad skirted around the woodpile and suddenly Eric stopped, staring at the logs.

Brad looked over his shoulder. "Is everything all—"

"No." Eric stared at him wide-eyed.

"What's wrong?"

He barely got the words out before Eric slammed Brad against the wall of the barn. Everything rattled with the force and two logs tumbled out of the pile and rolled across the yard.

"Eric, what the—" Brad gasped as Eric yanked Brad's head down and kissed him, grinding their mouths together.

Eric needed to feel Brad against him. He had one hand around the nape of his neck and the other cupping his ass, dragging the bear against him.

They kissed for long moments, Brad letting Eric control the connection of their bodies, their mouths, and it was good, but it wasn't enough. The layers of fabric between them acted as a barrier and he wanted them off. But he couldn't stop kissing Brad long enough to have that conversation.

Then Brad spun them around and it was Eric pressed up

against the wall, the rough wood digging into his back, Brad's mouth grinding down on his, his mustache and beard rasping along Eric's mouth. It was hot and heavy, but Brad cupped his jaw and held him tenderly as if Eric were something precious and not a stranger in his house. Eric took a long breath when Brad raised his head and stared down at him.

"Do you want to tell me what that was all about?" Brad asked.

"I wanted to know if it was real or something I lost when I lost my memory."

"The connection between us?"

Eric nodded. "You all describe it and I can't remember it up here." He tapped his head. "There's nothing but an empty space."

Brad cupped his jaw. "I'm sorry, my boy. It must be very hard for you, but you don't have to worry about recreating it if you don't want to. You're not staying here for any other reason than to get the book completed."

"You don't want to kiss me?"

Brad's leer told Eric he was talking nonsense. "I want to do a lot more than that with you. I want to take you into my bed and fuck you so hard, you forget your own name."

"Been there, done that," Eric pointed out.

Brad grimaced. "I'm real sorry. I never meant to say that."

Eric gave him the sweetest smile he could. "I'm sorry too. It was meant to be a joke, nothing more."

"Do you want to go to bed with me?" Brad asked, not letting go of Eric, but putting distance between them.

Eric didn't like that and pulled him closer. "I do," he whispered.

Brad stepped back and ran a hand through his hair making it more rumpled than it already was. "You're not making it easy for me to think straight," he grumbled and Eric laughed.

"I want you to kiss me. It's not complicated."

"I should do the right thing. You're vulnerable."

Eric narrowed his eyes. "I'm not a kid, Brad. I'm a grown man."

"But your accident—"

"I can't remember my life. I know how my dick works just fine."

"Still, we should take it slow," Brad insisted.

"Like we did before?" Eric asked sarcastically.

He saw Brad's eyes narrow and his lips press tight. Brad clearly didn't like being spoken to like that. Good. Eric didn't like the rejection. He knew Brad liked him, so why was the big guy saying no?

Then Brad expelled a long breath. "I'm not saying no, sweet boy."

"I'm not your boy," Eric said harshly and saw Brad flinch. He reached out to grasp Brad's hand, knowing he'd crossed a line. "I'm sorry, I don't know what's wrong with me." He grimaced because that wasn't true. "My temper is... not good. It's a side effect of the accident. I know you're trying to do the right thing. I'm just telling you that you don't have to treat me like I'm breakable."

Brad nodded, but Eric could see he wasn't sure. He sighed inwardly. Getting laid wasn't on the cards. He sought to change the subject.

"I want to see where Gruff found Lyle."

"The tree?"

Eric nodded. "It's one of my illustrations."

"I know where that is. We all do. We all visit it once a year." Brad sounded a bit choked up. "If Griff had walked past that tree..."

"Lyle would have died."

"I would never have met you."

"I'd have been disappeared," Eric said softly.

Brad held him closer. "It was fate looking out for you all."

"Will you show me?"

"Yeah, but let's get coats and gloves. The temperature is going to drop later."

Eric didn't bother to ask how he knew. Brad had lived on the mountains his whole life and understood the tang of the air and the vibrant colors of the sky. He wondered if he had that innate knowledge too, somewhere locked inside him.

They tramped back to the cabin, the silence between them still awkward. Eric prayed he'd not wrecked their relationship for good. He shrugged on the thicker jacket Brad insisted he wore, noticing Brad's heated eyes on him and relaxed a little. Brad liked Eric wearing his clothes and still wanted him.

"We could take my horse if you don't want to walk," Brad suggested. "She doesn't get enough of my attention."

"I'd like to walk this time," Eric said, holding out his hand.

Brad laced their fingers together and they walked back out into the mid-afternoon sun.

"Why was Griff out in the snow?" Eric asked.

"He was hunting. Our stores were low and we don't like that happening in case we get cut off. But it was dark, hunting hadn't been successful, and it was getting too cold to stay out there."

Eric hummed, forming the picture in his head, of the youngest Brenner brother out on the mountain alone.

They walked a long way into the trees and Eric wasn't sure of the route.

"How do you know which way to go? All the trees look alike."

Brad shrugged. "It's our mountain. We go all over it. It's what we do."

Eric held his hand a little tighter. "I lived on the same mountain and my world was very small."

"I know, sweetheart. I know."

"What do you think will happen to the theme park?"

"I don't know." Brad was silent for a few moments, and the only sound was the snow crunching under their boots and their breaths harsh in the icy air. "There's been talk of making it a school, but none of the boys want to go back there."

Eric shivered at the thought. "I thought I could see the place again, but the idea makes me want to vomit. I don't even remember it but just the thought of stepping back in there again..." He stopped, and Brad rubbed his back in soothing circles.

"You don't have to do anything you don't want to," Brad assured him. "Ah, there's the tree just there."

Eric followed where he was pointing.

"The one with the great big ribbon tied around it?" he asked dryly.

"There are a lot of trees," Brad said somewhat defensively. "We have to make sure we have the right one."

Eric gaped at him. "What was that about always knowing where you are?"

Brad couldn't help blushing. He put a finger over his lips. "Don't tell anyone."

"I promise," Eric declared with a smirk.

But then he turned to study the tree, imagining a boy stumbling through the darkness, his only guide the stars and moon, going knee deep in the snow. Lyle had been drugged. Eric knew that from articles he'd read about the family. He was unsteady on his feet. He'd tripped and knocked his head on one of the branches, then gone to his knees at the base of the tree.

He'd had maybe moments before he'd died of hypothermia, yet somehow Griff had found him and Eric's life, along with hundreds of other boys had been changed.

He imagined big bluff Gruff wandering by the tree, thinking of being home, and finding a body under the tree. One article he'd read said Lyle wasn't the first body they'd found and usually they left it to the sheriff to handle. What made it different for Gruff this time? Why did he pick up what he thought was a corpse and bring him back to the family home?

Eric must have asked the question out loud because Brad said, "Gruff thought he was a child. He couldn't leave him here for the predators to get him."

"But then he discovered the boy in his arms was still alive," Eric murmured.

"He did. And Lyle survived being disappeared and changed our lives forever."

Eric shivered, whether from the cold or what might have been he wasn't sure, and Brad said, "Let's go home."

They started the journey back, holding hands, a peacefulness between them Eric liked. Brad seemed to understand Eric didn't always want to talk.

After a while, Eric realized just how far they'd walked. "The tree is a long way from the cabin."

"It is," Brad agreed.

Eric looked over his shoulder at the way they'd come.

"And Gruff carried Lyle all the way. It's a good thing you guys are so huge."

"Men of the mountain."

Brad's pose and smirk made Eric laugh.

"Do you think you'll ever leave the mountain?" Eric asked.

Brad didn't answer for a moment. Then he said, "Only for the right boy."

Chapter Four

Brad

A day later, Brad was still tied up in knots over how he'd handled the incident, that's what he called it in his head. It wasn't a fight. It was him laying down boundaries for his boy. Not that Eric was his boy yet. Even on a temporary basis. They hadn't had that discussion. Brad sighed. Why had he stopped Eric when they clearly both wanted to bang each other's brains out? He should have done what he did before and drag Eric into the barn, pushed him over a bench, and bred that sweet little hole.

But Brad had stopped and he hadn't told Eric the full truth. It wasn't just about respecting Eric's vulnerability. Yes, he was vulnerable no matter what Eric said. But he also wanted to protect himself. From the moment Eric left him again, he knew he would be devastated. At that point he'd think about leaving the farm for good. He'd not be able to stay around his brothers and their boys. Their happiness would drown him. He'd be better to start a new life somewhere else. His big brother would hate it, but Damien had

Vinny now. He didn't need Brad moping around all the time.

In the meantime, he had to finish his project with Eric or he would lose his publishing deal. He'd winced when he'd finally gotten around to reading the emails from David Peterson. His publisher wasn't happy with him.

In need of something other than coffee, Brad walked into the kitchen to find Eric at the table with Jack and PJ.

Jack was saying, "All I wanted was something to eat. I was going to ask if I could wash the dishes for a meal. I stood behind this big guy and the next thing I remember, I wake up to find I'm on the floor in his arms."

"What happened?" Eric said, his eyes big. Then he saw Brad and flushed a lovely shade of pink.

Brad smirked as he kicked off his boots and headed over to the pan on the stove. They all shook their heads when he waved the ladle at them. He filled one of his mugs with hot chocolate and grinned as PJ spoke.

"I knocked him out."

"You hit him?" Eric sounded horrified.

But Jack chuckled. "PJ's a klutz. Never stand too close to him. Those arms move without warning."

PJ gave a rueful chuckle but he hugged Jack closer to him. "Unless it's you, darlin'. I'm never going to hurt you again."

Jack melted into his embrace and gave a happy sigh. He reached up to whisper, "Unless I ask for it, Daddy."

"So what happened then?" Eric asked, blushing pink again. He'd clearly heard Jack's whisper.

"I brought him home," PJ said.

"I never wanted to leave," Jack agreed. "They feed me here."

He shrieked as PJ tickled him. "No fair, Daddy."

Brad just rolled his eyes and sat down next to Eric. "You okay?" he asked quietly.

"I am. I've been talking to your brothers. It's been busy."

"Do you want to watch *Shrek* later?" Jack asked suddenly. "We're having movie night at our cabin. I bought popcorn."

Eric's eyes lit up. "Which one? I watched them all when I was in hospital. It was about all my brain could handle," he admitted with a grimace.

"We're gonna watch as many as we can," Jack said. "PJ loves Puss in Boots."

"No, *you* love Puss in Boots," PJ said with a chuckle. "You just love Antonio Banderas."

"You're not wrong there," Jack admitted. "But I do like my Daddy in his boots."

Brad's heart clenched at the look of adoration Jack gave his Daddy. He saw Eric gaze at them, then look away, biting his lip. He sighed, then smiled at Jack. "It's a great idea. I haven't watched a movie for ages."

"We should all be there."

"Are Alec and Jake here?" Brad asked.

The two had been away since the day before on a job they refused to talk about. Brad hoped it wasn't one that messed with their heads. He wasn't sure he liked their continued involvement with Josh Cooper. But he wasn't involved in their business so he had no say on the matter.

"They're on their way back," PJ apprised him. "They should be here in time for the movie. I should get back to work so I'm not late for my own movie night."

"Do you need help?" Brad asked him.

"Red and Harry are helping today." PJ winked. "You focus on your boy."

Eric made a choking noise.

Jack huffed. "Just think before you speak, Daddy, yeah?" He manhandled PJ out of the kitchen, a solid feat as PJ made three of him.

That left Brad and Eric carefully not staring at each other.

"I've never met a family like yours before," Eric said.

"I'd apologize but we're all the same," Brad said ruefully.

"I don't regret kissing you." Eric blurted it out as though he'd been having the conversation in his head.

"You don't?"

Eric shook his head fiercely. "Not for a minute. It was the hottest kiss of my life." He furrowed his brow. "Except maybe the one I don't remember?"

It was a question. He looked at Brad for help.

"Equal hotness," Brad assured him.

"Take me to bed, Daddy Braddy?"

Brad's heart stopped. "Don't use that name if you don't mean it."

Eric's gaze didn't waver.

"I mean it. But I can't promise forever."

Brad nodded. "I accept that." He stood and picked Eric up where he sat.

"What the?" Eric flailed before flinging his arms around Brad's neck. "You should put me down."

"Let's get one thing straight, my boy. I'm giving the orders, and if that means I want to carry you, that's what I'm going to do."

Brad stomped out of the kitchen with his boy, his cup of hot chocolate left forgotten and cooling on the pine table.

Brad had one agenda in mind. Make his boy come apart in his hands so he could put him back together with love and touches that whispered across his skin like butterflies in flight.

If Eric couldn't promise forever, then he would leave knowing he left behind the man who understood him the most.

Brad removed Eric's glasses and put them on the dresser. Then he slowly undressed Eric until the boy stood naked, afternoon sunlight streaming in through the window, gleaming across his winter-pale skin. It highlighted scars that had not been there the last time Eric stood in his room. He would kiss each scar, learning the damage that had been done to his boy, taking some of the pain inside himself.

Eric followed his gaze. "I guess you find them ugly."

Brad shook his head. "What was done to you is ugly. These scars are testament to your strength. They are you."

Eric gazed at him uncertainly. "You mean that?"

Brad pushed up his sleeves and held out his arms.

"I have scars too. Only these are through stupidity. I used not to be as careful with the chemicals when I started."

Eric studied the scars left behind by chemical burns. "I never noticed them before."

"It's why I wear long sleeves a lot," Brad admitted. He gently caressed one of the scars on Eric's chest. "You're beautiful."

"So are you," Eric husked. "Please, I need to see you too."

Brad stripped off his clothes until he was as naked as Eric. He tugged Eric into his arms. His boy's height was an advantage and he didn't have to dip his head far to capture Eric's lips. They kissed for a long while, their hands resting on each other's hips, their hard shafts rubbing delicious friction against each other. Brad wanted to stay like this forever, but soon Eric was rubbing against him with more urgency.

Brad liked to take his time, but his boy was young. Still, there was one way to deal with that.

Dropping to his knees, Brad swallowed Eric's cock to the root. Eric howled and gripped onto Brad's hair. It wouldn't take him long to get Eric coming down his throat. He sucked hard and Eric cried as delicious spurts of cum filled Brad's mouth. His boy tasted like home.

Eric's legs wobbled and Brad let him slip free from his mouth, and eased him to the bed.

"I want you, Daddy," Eric murmured, but he sounded sleepy, his eyes closed.

Brad wanted to fuck him but he had to remember his boy was still recovering from a serious accident.

"Please, Daddy."

Brad smiled down at him. "How about I straddle your face and you can suck me like that?"

Eric's eyes widened. "That's so hot."

Brad did as he suggested and straddled Eric's face only for his shaft to be swallowed into Eric's hungry mouth. He grabbed the headboard and groaned as Eric's tongue swept around his glans. His boy had a wicked mouth and he was using it to full effect. Whatever he'd forgotten, it wasn't how to give blow jobs. He looked down at Eric, his eyes closed, his lashes dark against his pale cheeks, a look of utter contentment on his face, sucking his cock like a boy sucking his pacifier. He'd seen that same look on Aaron's face. But he didn't want to think of his brother's boy now. His climax wasn't going to wait on his thoughts. Brad's balls tightened and he gripped onto the headboard.

"Make me come, boy," he ordered and Eric opened his eyes.

The suction grew stronger and Brad couldn't hold back, didn't want to hold back, crying out into the silence of the room as he spurted his seed into Eric's willing greedy mouth. They stayed like that as Eric sucked him dry.

Brad stared at a mark on the wall above the headboard. He couldn't let Eric leave. He couldn't.

* * *

PJ and Jack's cabin was packed. Jake and Alec had made it at the last moment. They looked tired but not wrecked which eased Brad's mind. He caught Damien studying them with the same intensity.

"Job go okay?" Gruff asked as he handed them beer bottles.

"Yeah," Jake said. "Not a rough one this time."

Alec nodded and raised his beer bottle. "To more like this one."

"Amen," Jake said fervently.

Brad caught Damien's eye and saw his brief nod. There would be a discussion at some point. That's how the family worked.

The brothers sat on chairs brought from the other cabins, their boys either on beanbags or on their laps.

Eric had started out on a beanbag, but had asked his Daddy if he could be hugged. Brad offered his arms and carefully avoided all his brothers' smirks. Eric settled onto his lap with a sigh, cuddling just as they had earlier.

They ended up going to sleep in each other's arms after making love and nearly missed movie night. It was only Gruff and Lyle talking outside his bedroom door that woke him up.

Eric sighed into his neck. "I thought you'd want to watch something with explosions."

Brad gave a wry chuckle. "I get enough of those at work. I like kids movies. I love Shrek."

"You just like Antonio Banderas," Eric said with a grin, clearly teasing him.

"What's not to like?" Brad thought the guy was as hot as hell and he rocked sexy boots.

He heard the soft snores whispering against his neck and kissed the top of Eric's head. His boy hadn't even made it to the opening of the first movie.

Eric

Eric finished the phone call with David Peterson at Peterson Press, threw his phone on his bed and hugged himself with glee. The publisher was thrilled Brad was cooperating at last and he loved the illustrations Eric had sent him. In the past two days, he'd managed to talk to three of the brothers and their boys, and a germ of an idea percolated through his mind. Brad had admitted he had no idea what illustrations should go with his poems, but Eric did. Peterson loved the idea. Now he just had to convince Brad.

He hadn't seen his Daddy since breakfast. Brad had been working in the barn and Eric had been at the kitchen table, making notes, sketching ideas, and talking on and off to Matt, Lyle, and Vinny. The boys were like his connection to his past and they told him stories he didn't remember but they swore were true. Maybe a few tears were shed too. But they had given him the idea for the theme of the illustrations.

He bounced off the bed and hurried down the stairs. He threw on the jacket and old boots he'd been wearing and stepped out into the late morning sunshine. The ice-cold breeze took his breath away.

"Wow," he managed as the cold seared down to his lungs.

Eric couldn't believe he'd lived on this mountain his whole life. Surely he'd remember the cold? He headed to Brad's barn but as he reached for the handle he heard Brad speak.

"No, it's not the right time."

"Don't be ridiculous," Gruff said. "You should tell him."

"I can't do that."

Eric leaned against the barn wall and listened to Brad argue with his brother.

Gruff made a half-huff, half-growl noise. At least, Eric assumed it was Gruff.

"Why are we all such idiots when it comes to our boys?"

"I'm not an idiot. I'm being respectful of Eric's needs."

Eric's eyes widened as he heard his name mentioned. What needs was he talking about? He blushed a little. Were they really talking about those kind of needs?

"And have you asked Eric what his needs are? Because I'm telling you, we've been through this with every brother and none of us bother to talk it through with our boys before we make a decision for them. And you know how that works out. The running away is getting tedious. At least you're the last one, I guess."

"Uh..."

Now Eric was confused. Brad never stopped asking Eric what he wanted. Sometimes Eric just wished Brad would take from him.

Gruff huffed. "Your boy looks at you like you hung the stars and the moon. He jumped you—again. You might not be the one who makes the first move in this relationship, but you've gotta let him know it's what you want too."

"It's not what I want," Brad yelled.

Eric's eyes filled with tears and he clutched at his stomach like he'd been punched in the gut. His Daddy didn't want him? Eric could barely breathe.

"Okay, big bro, give me a clue here." Gruff sounded confused. "You don't want Eric to be your boy?"

"Of course I want him to be my boy."

"So you do want Eric to agree to stay here forever and let you pound his cute ass into eternity?"

"You think he's got a cute ass?"

Oh wow, now Brad's voice had gone all growly and Daddy-like which did insane things to Eric's dick. He really loved it when Brad went into full Daddy mode. It didn't happen often enough as far as he was concerned.

Eric pushed down on his erection. He didn't want to walk into the barn with a full boner. How would he explain it?

"Don't be ridiculous. The only ass I care about is my boy's, particularly as I get the chance to pound it through the mattress every night. And you still haven't answered the question."

Brad sighed. "It's different for you and Lyle. You've been together for years now. This thing with Eric is still new and he doesn't remember the first time we were together."

Eric sniffled. He wished he could remember that moment. Everyone else had told him about it, but it stirred nothing in his memory.

"And he left you," Gruff said gently. "Is that what you're scared of? Him leaving you again?"

"It's just a job."

"It doesn't have to be. It could be forever."

Forever? Eric pressed himself against the wall of the barn so his knees didn't give away. He stared at the barn in front of him which housed all the freezers. Gruff didn't know what he was talking about.

It couldn't be forever. Could it? Eric felt dizzy at the thought.

"Who are you hiding from?" Damien asked.

He looked up to see Damien leaning against one of the barns. "I'm not, I just, I need to—"

"Then you overheard something that freaked you out," Damien suggested.

Eric nodded, wrapping his arms around himself.

"Do you want me to find your Daddy?" Damien's voice was gentle, as if he were trying not to freak him out even worse.

Eric pointed to the barn behind him. Damien nodded, strode over, and knocked on the door. At the yell to come in, he opened the door. Left behind in the cold, Eric rocked backward and forward, trying to calm the hell down.

Then Eric was swept against Brad's chest, his face pressed into Brad's soft beard.

"Hey, hey, tell me what's the matter, sweetheart." His voice was muffled but Eric understood what he said.

Sweetheart!

When did Brad start calling him that?

Eric licked his lips, spat out a mouthful of beard, and pressed his face into Brad's neck.

"Tell me what the matter is," Brad crooned.

Eric raised his head and stared into Brad's blue eyes. "What would you do if I said I wanted to leave?"

He saw Brad flinch, but his Daddy said, "I'd let you go, Eric. I wouldn't force you to stay." Brad narrowed his eyes. "Do you want to stay here or go? Did you hear my conversation with Gruff?"

"I did. You said you'd be respectful of my needs and

then got all growly with Daddy Gruff because he said I had a cute ass. Do you think my ass is cute?"

"Considering you've got a bite on one cheek and a handprint on the other, and I rimmed you out this morning, do you need to ask that question?" Brad growled.

Eric considered that. It probably was a stupid question. He flushed at the thought. Brad had jumped him as soon as they woke up. It had been super hot.

"Boy, what's freaking you out?"

"I don't know," Eric admitted. "I've only just met you...again."

"And you feel like the family is making decisions for you?"

Eric nodded mutely.

"It's okay. It's what we do." Brad stroked Eric's hair. "Honestly, we're nowhere near making decisions about a future together stage. We can just have fun and relax."

"You mean that?" Eric felt like he could breathe for the first time. "But you were telling Gruff—"

"It doesn't matter what I said to my brother," Brad insisted. "We've all had these conversations, sweetheart. It's what we do. The family wants me to settle down with my forever boy because they're all loved up."

"You don't want that?" Eric asked uncertainly. He caught Brad's hesitation. "Daddy?"

"Of course I do, but when it's right. What do you want, Eric?"

"I've no idea. Everything I had planned went south when I was hit by the truck. I thought I'd be going to school, but it doesn't look like that's going to happen." He snuggled into Brad's solid body.

"I've got ideas about that. Gruff could help you pass the entrance test for college. But in the meantime you could take a few courses online. It would get you used to studying again."

"What if my brain doesn't work?"

It was the thing that had bothered him in the dark of the night. He knew a lot of the family were taking online courses, but he'd wanted to attend college like he should have done. The Kingdom boys were being given funds to attend school. That had been his plan.

Brad stroked his head. "You don't have to do everything all at once, sweetheart. Take a deep breath. Talk about it to Gruff. Harry might have ideas on how to help your brain."

Eric wasn't sure about that. Harry seemed to know a lot about horses, but he wasn't sure how much he knew about wonky brains.

But he guessed he could relax enough not to have to make an immediate decision.

"Why were you outside the barn?" Brad asked suddenly.

Eric raised his head. "I've got an idea for your book. David loves it, but I wanted to make sure you do too."

Brad grimaced. "Can't you make it a surprise for me? Anything you do will be good."

Eric blinked at him. "You don't want to know what goes in your book?"

"I just write the poems. No one understands them."

"I do," Eric assured him. "And by the time you have my illustrations with them, so will everyone else."

Brad didn't look convinced, but Eric knew he was right. Brad was going to change the world with one book.

Chapter Five

Brad

Despite their discussion Eric looked so lost, Brad wrapped his arms around him for comfort. He was so different from the scared boys Lyle and Vinny had been, sometimes Brad forgot he was also a Kingdom boy and younger than them by a year or two. The past couple of years of independence had knocked the institutional behaviour from them. And the accident too. Eric's past had been erased. He couldn't remember who he was. Maybe in his case it was a good thing.

But not all the conditioning was erased. Brad could see it in the way he ate at mealtimes even if Eric wasn't aware of it. Even though food wasn't short, he would check all the time to make sure he was allowed to eat.

Eric shivered, disturbing Brad from his thoughts.

"Let's go back to the cabin," he suggested and Eric murmured his agreement.

"Is it always this cold? I can't remember."

Brad chuckled as they followed the path back to the

cabin. "Usually it's worse." He outright snorted at Eric's groan. "It's the way we roll here. Cold and freezing are permanent states of being."

"No wonder Red grumbles so much," Eric said. "He's from Florida. He probably thinks he's living in the North Pole."

"I'd love to see you tell him that." Eric gave him the side-eye and he laughed. "Not that brave, huh?"

"Have you met Red?"

"True." Brad grinned at him.

Eric slipped on ice and Brad lunged to catch him, swinging him up into his arms. Eric stared at him, wide-eyed and gasping. "What the hell?"

Brad smirked at him. "I was worried about you staying on your feet."

"Uh-huh," Eric said, infusing all the sarcasm he could into his voice. "You just want an excuse to hold me, don't you?"

"You think I need an excuse, boy?" Brad raised an eyebrow, loving the way Eric shivered.

He was teasing, playing with Eric, but he wasn't sure how he'd take it. Despite the fact they'd already slept together, he didn't want to assume anything.

"You don't need an excuse, Daddy."

Brad stopped, eased Eric to a standing position, and bent his head to kiss him. Eric wrapped his arms around Brad's neck. Brad swept his tongue along the seam of Eric's lips and his boy parted them eagerly, allowing Brad to dip in and duet with Eric's tongue. Eric groaned and the sound was captured between their mouths.

Brad raised his head and gazed down into his boy's beautiful eyes. "Let me take you back to my bedroom."

Nodding eagerly, Eric hung onto the collar of his coat. "I need you to fuck me, Daddy."

"I need to fuck you too."

"You could do it in the warm," Harry said.

Brad tore his gaze away from his boy and looked up... and up. Harry sat on the back of Thunder, grinning down at him. "We're going. Is Thunder okay?"

It was his way of checking after the yelling between Harry and Red a few days ago.

"It's...uh...resolved. We discovered this clever boy," Harry patted his glossy black neck, "had worked out how to escape from his stall. We strengthened the bolts and I had a lot of apologizing to do to Red and so did Damien. That was fun." He sighed and stared moodily over their heads. "Take Eric home. You'll freeze out here."

Brad nodded and patted Harry's leg. "He'll calm down."

"He loves you," Eric added.

Harry smiled at Eric. "He does. But he still deserves a lot of love from me for yelling at him. We'll eat in our home tonight."

"See you tomorrow, little bro," Brad said and led Eric down the path to the cabin.

"Do you think they'll be okay?" Eric asked.

"Harry and Red? They'll be fine. Red knows how important the horses are and Harry knows he has to make it right with his boy."

Eric nodded, but he didn't say any more as he tramped side by side with Brad who entangled their fingers together.

The cabin was quiet when they entered and for once there was no one in the kitchen.

"Do you want a drink?" Brad asked.

Eric shook his head. He licked his lips. "I want to go upstairs."

"We can do that."

They shed coats, hats, scarves, gloves, and boots. Endless layers preventing Brad doing what he really wanted to do, which was to get his boy naked and fuck him until he was a boneless, sated heap beneath him.

Finally they were done. Lyle would probably scold them for the mess but Brad didn't care. They ran together up the stairs and Eric tugged him toward his room.

"You don't want to go to my room?" Brad asked.

Eric flushed. "I've got stuff on the nightstand."

Brad grinned. His boy was prepared. "Lead on."

He liked undressing his boys. It was a thing. But Eric was ripping off his clothes as soon as they walked through the door.

He caught Brad watching him. "Come on," he ordered. "I need you naked now."

Brad stripped off his sweater. "Just remember who's in charge in the bedroom," he pointed out.

"As long as we're naked, I don't care who's in charge."

His boy had a touch of the bossy bottom. Brad would note that. Eric would soon find out that while he was the focus in the bedroom, it was Brad's rodeo.

When they were both naked, hard cocks dripping in anticipation, Brad pointed to the bed.

"On the bed, on your hands and knees."

Eric arched an eyebrow. "No foreplay?"

"We did that outside," Brad growled. "Now it's time for me to get acquainted again with your ass."

Eric squeaked and leaped onto the bed, head down, ass up as soon as he settled. Brad grunted. This was what he wanted. He pressed up behind Eric's fuzzy butt and ran his hands down Eric's back, sending a wave of goosebumps in their wake.

"Your hands are cold," Eric grumbled.

"They'll soon warm up on your hot body," Brad assured him.

"My Daddy is a meanie."

Brad smiled wickedly above his head. Oh yeah, he'd been called a lot worse, usually by boys in cock cages and standing naked in the corner with their Daddy's handprint on each butt cheek. Eric would learn. Brad sobered for a moment. He hoped they had time to learn.

"Brad?"

He saw Eric looking over his shoulder, his face pinched. "Is everything all right?"

Brad smiled at Eric and the tension eased. "I was thinking about all the things I want to do to you."

Eric flushed crimson. "I want you to do everything," he said hoarsely.

"I will, in time, but first you need to stay still."

Brad parted Eric's ass cheeks and licked a long line from his taut ball sac to his hole.

"Daddy!" Eric gasped, sounding shocked.

Brad did it again, then he licked around the hole. Eric shook and Brad grabbed his hips to keep him still. This was what he wanted, his boy's body, putty in his hands. He licked until the muscle relaxed enough for him to press in. His tongue darted in, then licked around the hole. He repeated the motion, and again, until Eric kept up a steady incoherent plea. He had no idea what Eric said, but it was interspersed with curse words. Brad decided to ignore those, this time. He had a pretty ball gag he could use in future.

Brad grabbed the lube, slicked two fingers, and pressed

into Eric's hole. He crooked his fingers. Eric cried out Brad's name. Bingo. He'd found his sweet spot.

Then Eric cried again as he spurted over the bed. Brad held Eric's dick as the spasms racked his body and he coated the comforter. Brad grinned, bit one ass cheek and spanked the other. His naughty boy had come without permission. How could he punish his boy in a way they'd both enjoy? Still thinking about it, Brad gloved up, slicked more lube on his dick and kissed Eric's hole with the tip of his dick. He sank his rock-hard shaft slowly into Eric's tight, greedy ass, watching every muscle twitch as Eric adapted to his cock inside him. He wouldn't rush. His boy would be begging to come again long before Brad let him. He wouldn't rush, he'd take his time, until his boy begged for his release.

Brad pulled out until just the head of his dick was in his boy's hole, then he pushed back in. Eric moaned and arched his back. Brad did it again, and again, watching Eric's hole swallow his shaft and then push against him. Eric moaned and squirmed. He did it again, and again, listening to the sounds Eric made, the way his body responded to every touch and movement.

Brad pulled out, his body trembling, and Eric cried out.

"Oh baby, I'm not finished with you yet."

He slicked his dick again and resumed his slow fucking, his dick encased in slick heat. Brad relished the sight of his dick sliding into the heat of his boy's ass. Brad pulled out slowly, then thrust in again. Eric pushed back, wanting more. Brad loved the fact Eric was always so eager to please. That had to be one of his favorite things about his boy.

Brad thrust in and out, his body aching to come. Eric whimpered, and Brad leaned down to whisper in his ear.

"Come for me again, sweet boy. I want to feel your ass spasm around my dick."

Eric cried out and came again. Brad grunted as his balls tightened and he came hard. Brad spilled his seed inside the condom and collapsed at the side of him, trying not to squash his boy. They lay panting together, hot and sweaty. When his limbs felt less like limp noodles, Brad cleaned them up and got another cloth to clean off Eric's belly. When he was done, Brad lay down and pulled Eric into his arms. Eric nuzzled in and Brad kissed his hair.

"I really need a shower," Eric said sleepily.

"Later," Brad said. "I need to hold you first."

Eric snuggled closer. "I like that idea. Hold me tight, Daddy."

Brad closed his eyes. It was one order he'd willingly obey.

Eric

The next morning, Eric woke to a gentle knock at the door. He raised his head, still half-asleep. "Yeah?" It was more of a husk. He coughed and tried to speak up. "Yeah? I'm awake."

"Eric, there's breakfast if you want it now." Brad was quiet, as if he didn't want to disturb him.

"Thanks. I'll be down."

"Okay." Brad sounded pleased.

Eric sat up and knuckled the sleep out of his eyes. It had to be early. It was still dark outside, dawn hadn't lightened the morning sky as yet.

He knew the brothers who worked on the farm started their day before dawn but he winced when he looked at the clock. It wasn't even 5:00am. Eric considered himself a lark, but this was too early even for him. He was tempted to roll over and go back to sleep, but Brad had asked if he wanted to go down, and he wanted to see his Daddy. Brad had stayed last night, but Eric hadn't heard him get up. He'd slept so hard in his Daddy's arms.

He also had to catch up with Jake and Alec, hoping he could see their office today. From the conversation around the table, they were involved in another large case which wasn't related to the Kingdom theme parks. He was curious to know what they were doing.

Eric dressed in clean clothes Lyle had left for him on the dresser. It was time he asked Lyle what he could do to help him. They'd all been so kind to him. He knew that was what they did, but he didn't want to take advantage of their generosity.

Nervously, Eric entered the kitchen, scanning it for Brad who wasn't to be seen. Vinny and Lyle were at the stove. Rexy sat nearby, looking up at them hopefully.

Lyle spotted him and smiled. "Hi Eric, breakfast is nearly ready."

Eric felt the familiar clench in his stomach at the thought of food, but he took a deep breath.

Lyle gave him a knowing smile. "Just eat what you can. PJ will eat the rest. Brad will be back in a moment. He got a call."

At this time in the morning?

His surprise must have shown because Lyle shrugged.

"No one keeps regular hours here."

"We were always up early in the theme park," Vinny said. "Don't you remember?"

Eric shook his head. "No."

Lyle elbowed Vinny who flinched. "I'm sorry, Eric. I didn't mean to hurt you."

"It's okay. I've just not got any memories of that time."

"I thought you'd get flashbacks," Lyle said.

"The doctors said the damage to my brain was too severe." Eric grimaced. "Either that or there's PTSD too. They had nothing to work from. I was a John Doe until they found the letter addressed to me. The Eric you know is a stranger to me, if you get my meaning."

"I'll try to find your records before you were put into the theme park," Lyle said. "There are still a few boys without records."

"You mean, you might know who I really am?"

The idea astounded Eric. After months of rehab and counselling, he'd just come to terms with knowing nothing about himself, and now he'd met the one family who knew who he was. He was also being offered the chance to find out what happened to him as a child that meant he'd ended up in foster care.

"Don't get your hopes up," Lyle warned. "It's really hit and miss."

"Do you two have your records?"

Lyle nodded. "I was six when I arrived so I have some memories of my parents." He looked wistful and Eric felt sorry for him.

"I have my birth certificate," Vinny said. "I really am a Vinny, Vincent."

"Some boys were called other names," Lyle said. "Red was a nickname, but he chose to keep it."

Eric had questions, but the kitchen door opened and everyone piled in, and the moment was lost.

"We're using the playroom this afternoon," Jake said as he spooned up oatmeal. "Anna needs time to decompress. Everyone's welcome."

Damien smiled. "I think we could do with that too."

There was a general murmur of assent around the table.

"I'll call Harry and see if he and Red want to join us," Alec said.

Brad turned to Eric. "You're welcome too, but don't feel pressured."

"Me?" Eric squeaked. He looked around the table. "You wouldn't mind me being there?"

PJ looked confused. "Why *wouldn't* you join us? You're one of us."

Eric opened his mouth and shut it again. He wasn't sure what to say to that. Brad just beamed from ear to ear.

After breakfast everyone went their separate ways. Eric told Brad he needed time to work. Alone at the kitchen table, Eric was able to focus on his illustrations. He'd talked to all the family and he had so many notes he was starting to lose track. But he read the notes and made a few sketches. He was so deep into his work, lunchtime arrived before he was ready.

Brad kissed the top of his head. "Going well?"

Eric sat back and rolled his shoulders. Brad dug his thumbs into Eric's knotted shoulder muscles.

Eric groaned. "This feels so good."

"You're welcome."

"Brad gives good massages," PJ rumbled and they all agreed.

Eric was just content to have his Daddy's hands on him.

Once lunch was finished, the couples peeled away to get ready for the playdate. Eric expected to head straight to the playroom, but Brad led him to his bedroom instead. Brad picked up a bag which was on his bed and handed it to Eric.

"I bought you something to wear in the playroom. You don't have to say yes. You don't have to change. There are no rules."

Eric blinked, then looked in the bag and pulled out the contents. "A onesie. You bought me a onesie?"

It was a blue onesie covered in rockets and stars.

"I know we haven't really discussed this, and I didn't know what you'd like. We can buy whatever you like another time, but you said you like looking up at the stars. I bought you briefs to match."

Eric looked in the bag again and spotted the briefs. He threw his arms around Brad. "It's perfect. Thank you, Daddy Braddy." He held it out. "Would you help me put it on?"

Brad nodded and took the onesie from him.

Suddenly nervous, which was ridiculous considering where Brad's tongue had been the previous night, he waited as Brad gently undid the snaps on his shirt and slid it off his shoulders. Then Brad slid his hands up under the T-shirt, seeking the warm skin. Eric hissed at the feel of his hands, the sensation going straight to his cock.

Brad undressed him until he stood naked, his cock hard and waving hello to his Daddy. Eric was a little embarrassed, but Brad seemed oblivious as he helped him into the briefs and tucked his hard dick away. His Daddy had done this many times before. Eric felt momentarily jealous, then sad his Daddy had never found a boy of his own.

Until now.

Maybe his Daddy had been waiting for the right boy.

It was a lot to think about as Eric helped him into the onesie and did up the snaps. It fit as if it were made for him.

Brad smiled at him. "You look perfect."

Eric turned to look at himself in the mirror. He bit his bottom lip. Did he look stupid? He was a nearly six feet tall man dressed in a onesie with rockets.

Then Brad stood behind him and enfolded him in his

embrace. For the first time Eric felt small. His Daddy engulfed him in his arms.

"How tall are you?" Eric murmured.

"I don't know," Brad admitted. "I stopped checking. I'm shorter than PJ and taller than Alec."

"PJ is a mammoth," Eric said, and then apologized quickly. "I'm sorry, Daddy. I didn't mean to be rude about Daddy PJ."

Brad just chuckled. "He is a mammoth, but that's not what's bothering you, is it?"

Eric hesitated.

Brad kissed his head. "Sweetheart, just tell me what you're thinking. I promise I won't shout. You can say anything you want here."

"Do I look silly? I'm a tall man, not a small boy like Vinny, or even Jack or Lyle."

Brad turned Eric to gaze down at him with such tenderness that the breath caught in Eric's throat. "You don't look silly. You look like my boy, the boy of my heart."

Chapter Six

Brad

"This is the playroom." Brad stood outside the closed door with Eric. "It used to be PJ's room until he moved out. We used to use the small room at the end, but with so many boys, they felt we needed a bigger room."

Eric narrowed his eyes. "They? Your brothers?"

Brad nodded.

"Why not you. Didn't you get a say?"

Brad licked his lips. "I don't come in here much. I didn't have a boy and I found it...difficult."

Eric's expression softened. "I understand. It must have been hard for you seeing all your brothers fall in love and settle down."

"I love the fact they're happy and settled," Brad hastened to say. He didn't want Eric to think he resented them or regretted their happiness at all.

Eric wrapped a hand around Brad's forearm. "You're a very kind man."

The door opened suddenly.

"But it's beyond time you joined us," PJ said and virtually hauled Brad and Eric, who was still attached to him, into the playroom.

"Geez, little brother," Brad grumbled. "We could come in by ourselves."

PJ rolled his eyes. "You were one step from running away."

Eric snorted.

Brad wasn't sure whether it was the 'little brother' to PJ who was a man mountain compared to the rest of them, or the fact he realized Brad was panicking. He'd been unexpectedly nervous which was ridiculous. It wasn't like he hadn't been in the little playroom. It was just he gave his brothers space to be with their boys.

But suddenly he was being hugged by his brothers and Eric was hauled over to join Lyle and Jack, and here he was, back in the family fold as if he'd never been gone.

Gruff tugged Brad down to sit next to him on the couch, and Brad was conscious that PJ had positioned himself between Brad and the door.

"I'm not going to run away," he assured them.

Gruff grunted and PJ just ignored him. Then Damien and Vinny, followed by Harry and Red came in, and Alec and Matt on his heels.

Harry took one look at him, saying, "About time." Then he flopped down into a wingback chair and tugged his boy onto his lap.

Jake and Anna arrived next. She was clearly nervous about Eric's reaction to her from the white-knuckled grip on her Daddy's hand, but Eric took her other hand and tugged her down next to him. Brad breathed easier at his boy's non-reaction.

Jake flexed his hand as he sat down in the spare chair. "She was very nervous."

"I explained about Anna," Brad said, "but he just shrugged and said, "Whatever." He was nervous about wearing the onesie. I think he needs time to find his boy. All the other boys are relaxed. Anna's nervousness might may him feel better."

"He's a little?" Jake asked.

"He thinks so. The thing is, his life only started last year. He's trying to work out what he is."

"Lyle will be glad for another little to play with," Gruff said.

PJ snorted. "Your boy just wants to hog all the trains."

At Gruff's sigh, Brad outright laughed. It was a never ending source of amusement that the sweetest man alive was a bratty little who hoarded toys and picked fights with the other boys if his Daddy wasn't looking.

Brad relaxed and watched Eric play with Anna and Lyle. He gave a long sigh and Gruff patted his shoulder.

"Good to have you with us, big brother. We missed you."

He'd missed them too.

"We'll have to take them to the Tin Bar soon." PJ said. "Now Vinny and Lyle and Aaron are old enough to visit."

Gruff chuckled. "Are you sure about Aaron? I'm not convinced he knows his real date of birth. Those Rapunzel years keep changing."

"Don't even go there," Jake said. "He's still using the fake ID. I've got to find out when Eric's birthday is. He might still be underage."

The owner maintained a strict twenty-one age restriction.

PJ groaned. "It would be ironic if you're the one who can't come after all that."

Brad smiled at his boy. "I can wait for him. It won't be long."

As if aware of his regard, Eric looked over to him. Brad smiled and received a shy smile in response. His boy wasn't comfortable yet, but they had time. Well, as long as Eric could stay here. He would have to have that conversation with Eric before it was too late.

"Stop it."

Brad blinked and found Damien leaning toward him. "Stop what?"

"You're imagining Eric driving down the mountain road for the last time, aren't you?"

His jaw dropped. "How did you know that?"

Damien just gave him the patented older brother 'you're being stupid' look. Only his older brother could make him feel that small. Except perhaps Gruff. And Harry. Did they all have that look?

"He's your boy," Damien said.

"You don't know that."

"We do," PJ assured him. "He's the boy of your heart."

Again, how did PJ, the least romantic of them all, come out with something like that? Then he saw PJ gazing at Jack with such adoration that maybe Brad didn't need to ask the question.

"You have a second chance with Eric. Don't lose it," Matt said, from his place at Alec's side.

All the brothers turned to stare at him and he blushed.

"Matty." Alec's tone was gentle but chiding.

Matt huffed but he gave an apologetic grimace. "I'm sorry, Daddy Brad. I forgot about the dynamic in here."

"It's okay, Matty," Brad said soothingly.

Of all the boys, Matt and Red struggled with regressing. Brad wasn't sure Matt really did. He always gave off the bratty sub vibe. But Matt was comforted by being with everyone. He craved it. It gave him a peace in his soul he didn't have usually. He'd admitted it in a rare moment of self-reflection in Brad's barn.

"You're thinking too much," Gruff said.

"You've all got an opinion," Brad grumbled, but they were right. Of course they were. They were his brothers.

Then he heard a "Mine! It's mine!"

Lyle glared furiously at Eric, clutching a blue engine to his chest. And Eric burst into tears. Brad was there in an instant, picking Eric up and taking him back to his seat to comfort him. Eric buried his heated face in the crook of Brad's neck.

"I've got you, my sweet boy," he crooned.

Gruff stood and loomed over his boy, hands on his hips. "Lyle Brenner, stand up." He held out his hand for the train. "Give me the engine."

Lyle clutched at it, but Gruff insisted, and he handed it over with a huff.

"In the corner for ten minutes," he ordered.

Lyle jutted out his bottom lip and didn't move. Gruff just raised an eyebrow. The whole room went silent as they watched the confrontation. Lyle huffed again, then stomped over to the corner, but before he did, he flicked a quick glance at Brad. And suddenly Brad understood. He'd been overwhelmed by his brothers, and Lyle gave him a distraction, even if he was the one to receive a punishment. What a clever, clever boy. He would thank him later.

Gruff sat down and winked at Brad. He knew exactly what had just happened.

Eric's sobbing calmed under Brad's gentle soothing and he stayed where he was, snuggled in Brad's arms.

"So..." Harry raised an eyebrow at his youngest brother. "Lyle Brenner?"

Gruff spread his hands. "We intended to get it all sorted but you know, things happened. But my boy is a Brenner by love as PJ said. So yeah, Lyle Brenner."

Lyle's shoulders twitched but he didn't turn around.

"It's a lovely idea," Harry said. "But we'll celebrate soon. We should have a party."

"Any excuse to get a lot of people up to the farm?" Alec laughed.

"I'd like to be a Brenner," Matt murmured in his ear. "I want to be yours."

There was nodding all around from the boys that Brad didn't expect. Even Eric twitched.

"Maybe it's time we made our commitments official," Damien suggested, smiling down at Vinny.

"Yes," Vinny agreed. "I'd like that."

Brad stroked Eric's back. Maybe they'd wait a little longer. He wasn't sure he could cope with six weddings when he didn't know if the boy in his arms was going to stay or go.

Eric

Eric was embarrassed by the fact he cried in front of everyone, but Brad had been there to hold him, and he'd stayed in Brad's arms for a long time. He was sure at one point he'd dozed off, but when he awoke, nothing seem to have changed, except he could see Lyle playing on the floor with Jack. Lyle's sudden outburst had thrown Eric, but no one else seemed bothered.

"Hey there," Brad murmured in his ear. "Are you awake now?"

"I am. I'm sorry, did I fall asleep?"

"Yeah. Not for long though."

Eric wriggled and Brad's arms came around him, to steady him. He didn't seem in any hurry to move his boy, but Eric had a need of a more pressing nature.

"I need to use the bathroom," he whispered.

"You need to go potty?" Brad asked.

Eric nodded, blushing furiously.

Brad set Eric on his feet, but didn't let go of his hand. He led Eric to the bathroom and shut the door behind him. Eric stared at him, not sure what to do. Did Brad expect him to go...with him standing there? He really needed to go. Eric tried not to fidget.

"I should have had this discussion with you earlier," Brad said. "I'll help you with the onesie. You can go alone, I'll wait outside. Or I can help you. Hold you," he added. "Or there is a potty there." He pointed to a blue potty sitting by the shower. "In future we could talk about diapers."

Eric nodded furiously, hopping from foot to foot. "Can you help me, Daddy Braddy. Now please."

To his relief, Brad unsnapped his onesie, turned Eric to face the pan, tugged his dick out of the briefs, and held his dick in his warm hand. It took a while for Eric to be able to relax enough to let go, but the relief when it happened was almost overwhelming.

"Good boy," Brad praised.

Eric hummed and focused on the liquid arcing into the pan. He had never done anything like this before. It seemed to go on forever but he had been desperate. Finally it trickled down to a dribble, then nothing. Brad gave him a shake and put him away again. He fastened the onesie and nudged him over to the sink to wash his hands. Brad did that for him too as though it were normal, then dried his hands and led him back into the playroom.

"Harry suggested we had dinner in here," Alec said. "He and PJ have gone to get the food."

Eric's belly rumbled loudly and his Daddy chuckled. "You like that idea?"

Eric rubbed his belly. "I do, Daddy. My tummy's rumbly." He didn't know how he could be hungry. He'd done nothing but eat since he arrived here.

Lyle came over to him, his head down, refusing to meet his gaze. "I'm sorry I was rude to you and didn't share. Here." He thrust out the blue locomotive.

Eric looked up at Brad who nodded. "Thanks. Let's play with it together."

Lyle beamed at him and took his hand, leading him to the mat where Jack and Anna sat. Vinny, Matt, and Red sat at a table. He wasn't sure what they were doing.

"I like the green engine best," Anna confided. "It has flowers on."

Lyle opened his mouth, then he looked over Eric's shoulder and just nodded. "Flowers are nice."

Eric was sure his Daddy had just given him a pointed look. "I like the red engine and the blue one."

Anna patted his hand. He noticed for the first time she clutched a pacifier in her other hand.

They played for a while. Eric was starting to get bored and look for something else to do when the door opened and PJ pushed a trolley into the room. Eric sniffed. Whatever it was on the plate, it smelled amazing.

"Time to clear up, boys," Harry announced cheerfully.

The boys grumbled but they tidied up, putting everything on the shelf, then sat at the table. Eric joined them, and Anna tugged him down beside her.

Brad looked at Eric. "Sometimes we feed our boys, but because it's late, it's just a normal dinner, but in here. You can ask for help or eat by yourself. I don't mind."

Eric stared at his hands. Brad was so laid back. Maybe too laid-back. Eric had a feeling he liked his Daddy to take charge.

Brad stroked Eric's cheek. "Let me feed my little boy."

It wasn't a question and Eric let out a sigh of relief. He didn't have to make a decision.

The dinner was mac 'n cheese for everyone and finger food for the boys. Vinny, Jack, and Matt helped themselves while Eric, Lyle, and Anna waited for their daddies. Red didn't seem to want to eat. He sat in Harry's arms and watched everyone else. Red caught Eric regarding him.

"I'm tired," he admitted. "Maybe I'll eat later."

Eric nodded. This was the one place in the world where people understood his food issues. None of the daddies pushed the boys to eat beyond what they could manage, although Gruff insisted Lyle eat at every meal. Lyle had admitted to Eric that he would forget to eat if he got the chance.

Eric squeaked as Brad picked him up like he was a child, sat down, and popped him on his lap. Eric fidgeted.

"Sit still," Brad ordered.

Eric blushed and did as he was told.

Brad slowly fed Eric and himself, while carrying on a heated discussion with PJ about the farm. No one else seemed to worry that the two men were disagreeing about something. Eric listened with interest because he hadn't ever been on a Christmas tree farm before, apart from the one time he didn't remember. It was hard to believe he had grown up so close to this place and never realised it existed. All he knew now was what Lyle and Vinny and Matt had told him.

The gist of the conversation appeared to be whether to continue the Christmas tree farm or not. At one point five brothers had worked on the farm, but the past two years had left PJ the only one working full time, with Harry and Brad pitching in where necessary. But Brad worked in his lab and Harry took care of the horses and was studying for something. Eric assumed it was something to do with animals.

Everyone else who had been part of the operation of the farm was involved in the aftermath of the Kingdom theme parks. Gruff was a full-time teacher, Damien seemed to be involved in something complicated to do with accounts that no one understood. Alec and Jake had their PI business.

PJ admitted that he couldn't continue without more help. None of the boys had shown any real interest in helping him. Jack was more interested in helping Alec and Jake. "I don't know what to do," he admitted. He sounded defeated.

"PJ, maybe it's time to admit we don't need to grow the trees. We could let it go," Brad said gently, the heat leaving his voice. "We've got other income streams now. We're not short of money."

"But what then? What can I do?" PJ demanded. "I was always the one working the farm. You guys all had other skills. I'm just the big lug. I can't study or teach. I can't be an investigator. Look at me. Can you imagine me following anyone?"

There was a loud snort although Eric wasn't sure who let it out.

PJ gave a snort of his own. "Exactly. I'm useless."

The playroom went quiet as his voice rose. Eric opened

his eyes a crack to see Jack clambering into PJ's lap, clearly wanting to give his Daddy comfort. Brad smoothed his hand down Eric's back, and Eric realized he was trying to soothe him. Eric snuggled in to show Brad he was fine.

"Little brother," Damien started. "You're not useless. You're just at a crossroads. We've found our paths. Now it's time to help you find yours. What do *you* want to do?"

"I don't know," PJ admitted. "I never had a choice before."

Eric filed that piece of information away. He knew from what their boys had said, the brothers had given up their dreams to keep the farm running.

"Then maybe you can take time to think about it. We'll help you keep the farm operational while you think about it."

"You kept working while we went away," Gruff said.

"You saved the world. I grew trees." And there was a bitterness PJ couldn't quite hide.

"We came back to a home, thanks to you," Jake said. "Alec and I have always had a family to come back to."

"Thanks, little bro." PJ sounded all choked up.

"We'll all help you until you decide," Vinny said.

Eric wondered what it was like to have a family like the Brenners. Who would be here for each other, no matter what. Could he ever have that?

Chapter Seven

Brad

Brad was quiet after the playroom. PJ's outburst had affected all of them, but Brad in particular hated any of his brothers being unhappy. He loved them and would carry the weight of the world on his shoulders to help them.

Eric took Brad's hand and led him into his bedroom, rather than Brad's. He took him over to the window and leaned against him as they stared out at the moon-lit sky.

"I wonder if I looked up at the moon and stars when I was in the theme park?" Eric murmured.

"I don't know," Brad admitted, sliding his arm around Eric's shoulder and holding him close. "I don't think you got much chance to look up at the stars. Now you get a second chance."

"Third chance," Eric corrected.

"Huh?" Brad was confused.

"My second chance was being rescued from the theme

park. My third chance is the life I have now. I can look up at the stars and know that I lived."

"You've survived so much," Brad said.

"And now I can live."

Eric tilted his head up at Brad and his face shone in the moonlight. "Take me to bed, Daddy?"

Brad turned and kissed him as he unsnapped the onesie. Time focusing on his boy would push away his melancholy. He pushed the onesie down until Eric could step out of it.

"Leave the briefs," he ordered as Eric went to push them down too.

He picked Eric up in his arms and gently laid him on the bed.

"You're always so gentle with me," Eric murmured.

"You deserve it."

"Thank you." Eric pulled him down for a kiss.

Brad balanced on his hands, trying not to squash his boy.

"But I wouldn't mind a little rough too." Eric smirked, his expression clear even in the moonlit room.

"Cheeky brat," Brad said fondly, popping him on the hip as he couldn't reach his butt and kissing him again before he stood and stripped off his clothes.

When they were both naked apart from Eric's briefs, they lay on the bed facing each other. Brad sucked in his breath at how beautiful his boy was in the moonlight. "You look otherworldly, ethereal." He traced a path from his cheek to his lips.

"It hides the scars," Eric said and there was a hint of bitterness in his voice.

"Your scars are part of you and beautiful," Brad chided.

No one got to demean his boy, not even Eric.

"Only you would see beauty in imperfections."

Brad opened his mouth and then closed it again. He would ask Vinny to talk to Eric about the lines that mapped his back from the beatings he'd received and how Damien loved each one with his lips and hands. But that was for another time. Now he wanted to make love to his boy.

He leaned over Eric and picked up the lube from the nightstand, placing the tube on the pillow. First, he had something he needed to do. Brad wriggled down the bed until he was nose to cock, Eric's shaft just covered by a thin layer of blue cotton. He mouthed over the bulge in his briefs, gently sucking the flavor.

Eric buried his hands in Brad's hair. "Oh. Daddy. I..."

Brad raised his head. "Hush, boy. This is my time. You lie there like a good boy and let me explore."

"I want to suck you too," Eric begged. "At the same time. Please, Daddy."

Brad thought about that for a moment. That seemed like a good idea too.

He sucked thoughtfully on the cotton. "Okay, but when I'm ready, boy. Not before."

He smiled as Eric whimpered.

Brad sucked hard on the briefs, then dragged the cotton down Eric's thighs. Eric's cock sprang free and pointed at Brad's face. The pretty plump head glistened with pre-cum. Oh yeah. He wanted that in his mouth, and he was damn sure Eric wanted to give it to him.

He licked across the slit, tasting the sticky fluid. It was like a drug to his senses, and he wanted more. He plunged his lips over the head, swallowing the silky liquid, then took it deep into his throat, his lips sliding down the shaft.

Eric moaned and arched his back, his hands now buried

in Brad's hair. Brad began to bob his head, sliding Eric's hot and heavy dick in and out of his mouth. He wanted to taste more, need to feel Eric spilling down his throat.

"Daddy, I want to suck you too," Eric begged, tugging on Brad's hair.

Brad thought for a moment, then he said, "I'll lie on the bed, and you straddle my face."

"God yes," Eric said hoarsely.

Brad lay back, and Eric quickly straddled his head. "Oh God, Daddy," he moaned, his hands on Brad's thighs. He breathed warm air across the head of Brad's dick and sucked him in, licking and nibbling the thick shaft.

Brad's tongue caressed the underside of Eric's cock as it slid into his mouth. He was going to give Eric the blow job of his life. His lips sealed around the shaft, and he started to suck, gently at first then more vigorously. Eric moaned and the vibrations from his mouth danced across the sensitive glans. Brad sucked harder and Eric's cock jerked in his mouth.

"Yes, Daddy, yes." Eric moaned again, clearly unable to focus on sucking Brad's cock.

Using his lips and tongue, Brad laved the glans making Eric cry out around Brad's cock.

"I'm coming," Eric gasped before his cock jerked and hot cum flooded Brad's mouth.

Brad held Eric's shaking body, his lips firmly around the shaft, and swallowed the sweet cum until the last drop.

Eric pressed a kiss to the tip of Brad's dick. "Your turn, please Daddy."

"Yes, boy, make me come."

He took Brad's dick deeper, his tongue sliding across the sensitive head. He licked the slit and then engulfed the crown. Brad shot his load into Eric's mouth and Eric swallowed it all before collapsing on top of him, his face hot against Brad's thigh and his softening cock.

Brad patted the sweet butt in his face gently, too sated and boneless to do anything except lie there and grin up at the ceiling.

Eventually Eric sighed. "I must be heavy."

"You're perfect," Brad assured him.

But Eric kissed his dick and wriggled off him, turning to rejoin Brad on the pillow. They lay together, sweat cooling on their skin. Brad traced down the bumps of Eric's spine. His boy was thin. Not like Lyle and Vinny, or even Red. But he could do with feeding up. Eric had admitted he'd gone without meals so he could buy his art materials. If—when—Eric left, he would have money for both. He wouldn't go without again.

Eric yawned, stretched, and wriggled against him. "Hey." He pressed a kiss to Brad's nipple.

Brad grinned at him. His boy had a thing about his nipples. "I thought you were asleep."

"I was, at least I was dozing," Eric said in a sleepy voice. You wear me out."

"You wear me out too. I'm twice your age."

Eric raised his head and gazed up at Brad, his stormy grey eyes troubled. "Is the age gap going to be an issue?"

Brad cupped Eric's neat butt. "Not for me. It's kinda normal in our family. Damien and Vinny have about the same age difference. I've had boys of all ages, older and younger."

Eric growled but he lowered his head onto Brad's chest.

Maybe mentioning other boys wasn't the most tactful thing he could have done, but it made a point. Brad was all about the boy, not the specifications.

Eric sighed, blowing hot air across Brad's skin. "It's hard for me, you know? You've been a Daddy your entire life."

Brad hugged him close. "I have. I realized what I was a lot earlier than most of my brothers. But it's a learning curve and every boy is different. I don't expect you to be experienced. I just want you to work with me."

"Did you ever...with a boy...twice?" Eric looked up to catch his gaze.

"Are you asking if there was someone special?"

Eric bit his lip and nodded.

"I had someone on and off for a long time but in the end, we were only ever going to be part-time Daddy and boy, and that's not what either of us wanted. He traveled the world. I wanted to stay on the farm."

Eric nodded and Brad could see him thinking, processing what Brad had said. "Your family comes first."

"Yes and no."

Eric squinted. "What do you mean?"

"I've never met a boy I would put before my family."

"Oh." Eric settled down again. Then he sat up. "What about me?"

"I think it's a discussion we should have later."

Brad knew he'd tumbled into lust and then maybe love with Eric. But stepping away from his family was another matter.

Eric flopped back against the pillows. "I'm glad you said that."

"You are?"

"If you'd declared your undying love for me and said you were going to follow me for eternity I'd have been worried."

Brad snorted. "Too soon?"

"Yeah."

Brad chuckled, maybe a little relieved. All the boys were different. Vinny had a leash around Damien's heart from the moment they met whereas Red would bolt back to Florida if he could, even now. His undying love for Harry kept him in his Daddy's arms.

He rolled Eric onto his back and locked Eric's stormy gaze with his. "I don't want you to leave yet. I want to get to know you until you have to go. Can we do that?"

"Until the next job? Okay."

Brad nodded, knowing he had a breathing space. Eric was still new to the scene. He probably wouldn't get another job immediately.

Eric pulled him down for a kiss. As their mouth parted, he said, "Teach me about being a boy, Daddy Braddy?"

"I'll teach you everything you need to know," Brad promised, and kissed him again.

* * *

Brad's stomach rumbled. He'd been working all morning, having promised his boy over breakfast they would spend the afternoon together. Eric had kissed Brad's cheek and told him not to rush. He had ideas he needed to sketch before he lost them. Brad got a little growly when he mentioned Peterson was harassing him to get the job down. Eric blushed and rolled his eyes, but Brad saw how much he liked the possessive growl. His boy had a very expressive face.

He picked up his phone to check the time and saw the screen light up. It was a message from Matt.

9-1-1

Kitchen

Rapunzel

Brad blinked at the distress call. Rapunzel? Had Matt lost his mind? Was something wrong with Aaron?

Eric! His boy was there!

His mind racing, Brad shut everything down safely, chemicals locked away, even though he chafed at the delay. His brothers would be there. He had to go through the correct procedures before he could leave the lab. He couldn't afford to take chances.

The first second he could, he charged out of his barn as though a bull was after him. He slipped, sliding on the ice and stumbled. He recovered his footing and kept going.

I can't lose him now. I've only just found him.

Then he heard the sound of a single shot and Brad's... world...stopped.

Eric

"Antonio, I've found you at last."

They all turned to see a woman in the doorway. Eric thought she looked wild, as if she had just come off the mountain, but then he studied her closer and realized that was an illusion because of her unkempt graying hair and wild blue eyes. Under a red wrap, she wore a dress Eric recognized as vintage Chanel. He'd seen the same dress in an article he'd read the previous month. And her pointed shoes, more suitable to city life than a farm on a mountain, were definitely Prada. But she was filthy dirty. Skin, hair, dress, and shoes. Either life had been unkind to her or she was incapable of looking after herself.

Vinny grabbed Rex who was growling, teeth drawn back, and squinted at the strange woman. "Who are you?"

Then Eric watched the blood drain from Aaron's face.

"Mom?"

The woman's attention snapped to Aaron, and it was if no one else was in the room, her whole focus was on him. "Antonio!"

"I'm not Antonio, I'm Aaron."

Aaron got to his feet, but in an instant Red and Jack were by his side, Jack's arms around him, supporting him, Red's hand around Aaron's bicep. They were both muttering in Aaron's ears but it was unclear whether he heard a word they said.

"Antonio, baby, I've been looking for you for so long and now I've found you."

"Who's this, Aaron?" Lyle asked, his tone calm.

Eric spotted Matt slipping out the back and he was sure Matt was sending an SOS to everyone. He had no idea where any of the brothers were except Brad who was in the barn, but they'd get here. He was sure of that.

"It's my mom," Aaron said, his voice thin and reedy.

Eric knew a little of his story. Of being locked up for years, shut away from society. He talked little about his Rapunzel years as he called them, too painful to recall. But they all knew he was younger than his paperwork said and he'd been working in bars when he was barely fourteen.

From his pale face and wide, frightened eyes now,

Aaron was terrified. His greatest nightmare had come true, his past had returned to drag him back.

"Baby, where have you been?"

She rushed forward to hold him, but Eric was moving before he thought about it, standing between Aaron and the woman.

"I don't know who you are, lady, but you don't belong here."

The woman scowled at him. "Stand aside. I'm going to take my son home."

Eric shook his head. "He doesn't want you here."

Then Vinny and Lyle were by his side, a solid force protecting one of their own. Rexy barked, the sound echoing in the kitchen.

"Shut the damn dog up," she snapped.

Eric waited for Vinny to explode as he did when anyone was mean to his dog, but he evidently thought better of it and hushed him. Rexy gave an uncertain whimper but he settled against Vinny's legs.

"Please leave," Lyle said. "You're not welcome here."

But the woman ignored him and tried to peer around them to see Aaron. "Antonio. Come home, baby, Momma forgives you."

"Forgive *me*? You forgive *me*?" Aaron's voice was so harsh, it was almost painful to listen to. "What for?"

"For running away from me, of course." The woman smiled at him indulgently as though he were still a child. "I know you didn't mean to scare me. We'll go home and have French toast to eat in the nursery."

"You're barking, lady," Jack muttered behind Eric.

Eric agreed with him.

The woman swayed again, and Eric tensed, waiting to see what she'd do. But Aaron spoke then.

"I'm not going with you. I'm an adult. You're never going to lock me up in that bedroom again."

"Don't be silly. You're thirteen. You can't look after yourself. You need your momma."

The harsh sound that tore out of Aaron's throat made Eric wince. "I was thirteen when I ran away from you, Mom. I'm...twenty-two now."

Eric knew he was having to work out his Rapunzel years, not the age he told everyone he was.

But the woman's smile grew even more indulgent. "Don't be silly. You only ran away last week. Now come with Momma. Say thank you to the nice men, but it's time to go."

"I'm not going with you." It was almost a scream.

She scowled. "No need for a tantrum, Antonio."

Then Matt pushed in front of Eric. "Go now. I've called the sheriff."

Eric was surprised at that announcement as the sheriff's office was in town and over an hour away, and the brothers were all on the farm. But Aaron's mom didn't know either of those things.

"You stole my son. He'll arrest you for child endangerment."

Eric had to hold back a laugh. It was ridiculous as Aaron was an adult.

"Child endangerment," Aaron screeched. He shoved between Eric and Lyle and stared at his mother. "You kept me locked up for years. You denied me food, family, friends. I never spoke to anyone except you. You made my life a misery."

"Now, now, no need to shout, Tonio."

"My name is Aaron."

His mother scowled. "I made sure you were safe, boy."

Eric flinched as did all the others. 'Boy' was sacred in their home and no one used the term lightly.

"The world is dangerous. I always made sure you were safe, didn't I?" Now her tone was coaxing as if she were trying to be reasonable and why was Aaron being so annoying. "I protected you."

"You imprisoned me," Aaron said bitterly. "I didn't start to live until I ran away from you." Tears rolled down his cheeks and he wiped them away impatiently.

She gasped as if he'd wounded her. "How can you be so mean to your momma? We had each other."

Aaron gave a bitter laugh. "I had years of staring at four walls. You weren't with me."

Eric pushed Aaron into Jack's arms. "Just stay there, okay?"

Aaron nodded, and once again he was enclosed in a Jack and Red hug.

"I want my Daddy," Aaron murmured.

Eric wanted his too. Where the hell were they? He'd seen them rush en masse into the cabin before and that was just when Lyle called them in for dinner.

"Time to go," Matt barked at her. "You're not welcome here."

Then suddenly everything went crazy. She pulled out a gun and pointed it at Matt. "You can shut up or I'll shoot you."

Eric knew very little about guns, except this was big and black, and she was still swaying so they really needed not to trigger her, because who knew where she'd shoot.

"What the fuck, Mom?" Aaron's voice cracked and there was no joke about the swear jar. "Where did you get a gun?"

"I've always had a gun, dear." And now she wasn't

swaying. Her aim was deadly accurate and it was pointed at the center of Matt's chest.

"Mom, no!" Aaron yelled, pulling away from his friends' hug. "I'm not gonna let her do this. Let me go. I've got to go with her, I can't let Matt be hurt."

That was aimed at someone, Red, maybe. Eric's suspicion was confirmed when Red hissed, "You're ours, not hers. You're not going anywhere until Jake gets here."

She didn't take her eyes off Matt. "You come with me, son, and no one gets hurt."

Son was better than boy, Eric guessed.

"Put the gun down," Damien barked from the door to the hallway.

"Daddy," Vinny whimpered, but for once, Damien's attention was on someone else.

Her eyes went wide but she didn't take her focus away from Matt.

"Put the gun down," PJ boomed from behind her. "I've got a shotgun aimed between your shoulder blades."

Eric had to give her credit for nerves of steel. She didn't flinch at all.

"You won't shoot me," she declared. "You don't want to risk your boys."

She laughed as they all stared at her. "You think I didn't do my homework? I found out exactly who my son's been living with. You think the authorities aren't going to be interested in your den of iniquity?"

"What's a den of iniquity?" Vinny hissed to Lyle.

"I've no idea," Lyle admitted. "But the authorities know all about us. Seven couples living together, all of age."

Her face scrunched up. "It's disgusting."

"Locking your child up is disgusting," Eric said. "You can't take the higher ground, lady."

"You try to ruin our lives and Aaron can talk about his, and believe me, we know more than you'll ever want to get out," Matt agreed.

"Aaron is mine," Jake said.

Eric couldn't see him but he sounded as cold and implacable as Eric had ever heard him. He heard the whimper that told him Aaron was safely in his Daddy's arms.

Where's my Daddy?

Eric really needed Brad.

"Aaron is mine, he is home," Jake informed her. "You need to get the hell out of here."

The gun waved for a second.

"Now!" Damien boomed.

Before PJ could grab her, she fired the gun. It was chaos for a moment.

Eric stumbled back, but he stayed on his feet. Then PJ grabbed her as Brad burst into the kitchen.

"Where's my boy," he bellowed.

Eric tried to reach him but there were too many men between them.

Aaron's mom shrieked loudly until Alec had her on the ground, hands behind her back.

"You'll never try to hurt my boy again," Alec snarled.

Eric was sure he used a word for her that was banned in the cabin but if he did, no one cared.

Eric turned to find Aaron enfolded in Jake's arms.

Then Red looked at Eric and his expression changed.

"You're bleeding!"

Eric looked down and saw the blood soaking through the flannel of his right sleeve. Suddenly his arm hurt, a lot.

"Brad! Harry! Get over here!" Red bellowed so loudly it hurt Eric's ears.

Brad charged over to him. Eric tried to hold his arms out but they didn't seem to want to work. As Brad reached him, his knees buckled.

"Think...I've...been...shot...Daddy."

Chapter Eight

Brad

"If you don't put your butt on that seat and stop pacing, I'm going to get PJ to drive you home," Alec snapped at Brad.

"Try it," Brad snarled and went back to pacing the hospital waiting room.

Five steps, turn, ten steps, turn, five steps, turn, ten steps turn, rinse, repeat.

He wasn't going to be separated from his boy under any circumstances. It was bad enough he had to wait here, apart from him. He'd wanted to go in, to sit with Eric while he was treated, but the hospital staff had whisked his boy away and left Brad there, the double doors separating them.

Five steps, turn...

Alec sprang to his feet, snarled back and they glared at each other, almost toe to toe.

In the back of his mind, Brad hated this, hated confrontations with his brother. It was why he spent so much time in his barn. And he loved Alec, but right now he could kill him.

"Sit down, both of you," Damien said as he walked in, Vinny at his side. "Your boy is fine, you know that. Quit pacing, Brad, and drink this swill they call coffee. Alec, leave him alone. I know you're freaked about Matt but nothing happened to him."

"It could have," Alec growled as he accepted a cup from Vinny. "She pointed her gun at him."

"And he shot Eric," Brad snapped.

Alec seemed to crumple. Damien steered him to a seat away from Brad. "I know, I'm sorry."

Brad sipped at the coffee, pulled a face at the taste. He deflated at Alec's apology. He knew Alec was freaking out, for the same reason he was. Their boys had been in danger and they'd all been scared she would fire at them. He slumped down next to Alec. "Matt's all right, Alec."

Alec grunted. "I keep seeing that bi...woman aiming her gun at my boy. It's all I can see."

Brad put his arm around Alec's shoulders and hugged him. "He's okay. You'll make sure of that."

He had a feeling there would be another time of healing at the farm. Their home had been violated, again.

"I should be comforting you," Alec admitted, putting down the takeout cup. "This is vile," he muttered.

"My boy is...I don't know what he is, but I'm gonna find out."

He hated the fact he wasn't allowed to be with Eric because he wasn't Eric's named contact. If it was any one of the brothers, they would have let him in, but Eric was an outsider. Brad wondered if he could persuade Eric to put him down as his emergency contact, so if anything happened to Eric, wherever he was, someone would call him.

Some of the hospital staff were more helpful than others. He knew a couple of the nurses and they would have let him in, but today was not their day and the family had all been shooed to a waiting room while Eric was examined and stitched up.

Brad knew Eric was fine. It was a graze, nothing more. The bullet embedded itself in the cabinet behind Eric. All he needed was stitches. Harry could have done it, but once the sheriff's office had gotten involved, they insisted Eric went to the local clinic. There'd been was a collective grimace by the brothers, and Eric panicked as he had no health insurance, but Lyle said he would handle it as Eric was a Kingdom boy.

Brad had held Eric in his arms and pressed a towel to the wound all the way down the mountain road while PJ drove and Alec held Matt in his arms. Brad wasn't sure why Alec and Matt were there, but they insisted.

Eric had been brave and insisted he was fine, but he'd buried his face in the crook of Brad's neck and Brad had felt him shake. He'd finally admitted he hated the sight of blood. Brad had unwrapped his scarf and wrapped it around his arm, hiding the blood-soaked towel. The scarf had gone in with Eric. He didn't expect to see it again. Again, one of those random thoughts. The scarf had been knitted by his mom. He was sad to lose it, but Eric mattered more.

"What's happening back home?" he asked Damien.

"Aaron's mom is in custody. The sheriff's office has the gun and the bullet. They're taking statements from everyone. Matt needs to stop in at the sheriff's office on the way home to give his statement."

Alec grunted.

"Where is he?" Vinny asked.

"He's outside, talking to Josh Cooper. He refused to let me talk to him. Said I was too shouty and I needed to calm the fuck down. I'm going to spank his ass later for that and the swearing."

No one said anything. Not even an eye roll.

"How's Aaron?" Brad asked.

"He was devastated. And he's panicking that Eric is badly hurt. I think he's gonna be baking a lot."

Vinny whimpered. Aaron's baking left a lot to be desired.

"Maybe you could help him?" Brad suggested. "How did his mom find him?" He had been thinking about that all afternoon.

"It was the media storm of publicity after the boys were rescued. Aaron was in one of the photos. You know he usually tries to hide, but he didn't know about this one. She spotted him by chance. She'd been looking for him since he ran away."

"Did she say why she locked him up?" Alec asked.

"He was her precious, magical boy. He needed to be kept safe from the world. The woman is as crazy as a fruit loop, and you know I don't say that about many people. She needs serious help."

"Poor Aaron," Brad said.

They were so absorbed with the Kingdom boys, they tended to forget Aaron had suffered another form of abuse.

"I think he's also frightened she'll come after him again," Damien said. "And Jake is scared he'll wake up one morning and find Aaron gone because he thinks he needs to protect us."

"That's why Matt is talking to Josh Cooper, isn't he? To see if he can intervene?"

Alec wrinkled his nose. "He doesn't know who else to talk to. The man seems to have a magic ticket to speak to everyone."

"Whatever he can do, we need to convince Aaron he's part of the family and he isn't going anywhere," Damien said.

"I'll bolt every door if necessary," Brad suggested.

"I'll get him to peel potatoes," Vinny added. They all smiled at him. Time spent over the potatoes was the best therapy they could have.

But that reminded Brad of his boy. Where was he? Why was it taking so long to put in a few stitches?

Then the door opened. A pale-faced Eric walked in, a nurse at his back. Brad was on his feet in an instant, rushing over to him.

"Are you all right, sweetheart?"

Eric gave him a wan smile. "I'm fine. Just a few stitches."

"Make sure he keeps them dry and no drawing for a few days. He needs to rest that arm," the nurse insisted.

"I'll make sure he rests," Brad assured her. He would tie Eric to the bed if necessary. Maybe some intense Daddy and boy time would keep Eric occupied while he couldn't work.

But Eric didn't look happy. "What if the publisher gets upset and tries to replace me?"

"We'll deal with that if it happens," Brad soothed him, drawing him into his arms.

Right now, the book was the last thing on his mind. All he wanted to do was take Eric home and take him to bed, shutting out the world behind them.

The nurse handed Brad a bag. "Fresh dressings if he

needs them and your scarf is in there. Eric insisted we kept it, although it's covered in blood."

"Thanks, my boy," Brad whispered in Eric's ear and took the bag. "Is he free to go?"

"Yes." The nurse smiled at Eric. "You were very lucky. Don't get shot again," she teased.

"I'll try not to," he assured her.

Then he turned to Brad. "Take me home, Da...take me home?"

Eric

He was going home, in his Daddy's arms. It didn't matter that it was a temporary arrangement. His Daddy Braddy was holding him like he was never going to let him go, his solid, meaty arms a welcome embrace. Eric pressed his nose into Brad's neck. He smelled of the chemicals he'd been using before the incident, but Eric inhaled deeper, smelling Brad's spicy soap and his earthy scent beneath that.

PJ, who appeared when Alec called, drove them back. Eric dozed on Brad's shoulder, as the others talked. Brad stayed silent, apart from the occasional hum in Eric's ear. He seemed to be thinking about something.

Another time, eternally curious, Eric might have queried what Brad was thinking about, but the adrenaline that had propelled him since he challenged Aaron's mom had crashed, now he just felt sore and tired. All he wanted was Brad.

"We're gonna spend time in the playroom later," PJ said. "Will you join us?"

It took a while for Brad to seem to realize they were talking to him. "Yeah, maybe, I don't know. I think we could do with some time to ourselves, yeah?"

"I think Jake is asking for Aaron," Alec admitted. "He needs to know he's still part of the family."

"I'll see how Eric feels," Brad said, his voice firm.

PJ snorted. "You've got it bad, big brother."

Eric expected Brad to laugh it off, but he didn't. Instead he said, his voice so soft Eric barely heard it, "Yeah, I think I have."

"That's nice," Matt said. "You deserve it. And Eric deserves a Daddy who focuses on him. It must be hard for him not remembering anything."

Brad sighed under Eric's cheek. "I don't know how to make that up to him. I don't know what I can give him."

"He needs you," PJ rumbled. "That's all he needs."

They fell silent then, the conversation exhausted to Eric's relief, the only noise the rumble of the tires on the road and PJ's off-key hum. Eric kept quiet, not knowing if Brad had been aware he heard everything. One thing he did know was that PJ was a lot more perceptive than the big man appeared. Eric desperately needed his Daddy, even if it was only for a short while. It was getting harder and harder to think about leaving though. Could he give up his dream to spend the rest of his life on the mountain?

* * *

"Sweetheart," Brad whispered. "We're home."

Eric raised his head, blinking sleepily at him. They were back at the cabin. It was late and the sun had set sometime on the journey. The truck was empty apart from the two of them.

"I guess I did fall asleep after all."

"You did." Brad's lips twitched and Eric guessed he'd

just given himself away. "I thought you might need some time to wake up. Let's go inside."

Eric yawned and nodded, appreciating his consideration. He stumbled out of the car and rolled his shoulders, trying to ease the ache in his muscles, then flinched as his arm protested.

"Ow!"

"Careful," Brad rumbled. "You don't want to tear the stitches."

Eric nodded contritely. The last thing he wanted to do was drive all the way back to the clinic. Every muscle in his body ached. He just wanted to collapse into bed. Maybe his Daddy would cuddle him for a while.

"I'm not awake," he muttered.

"Come inside and I'll help you relax," Brad said.

Eric let himself be herded toward the door, Brad's hand on his lower back.

"It's gonna be loud in there," Brad warned. "Prepare to be mobbed."

The thought was alarming, but then it was the first time anyone cared if he was alive or dead.

He took a deep breath and stepped into the kitchen. All eyes turned to him, then Lyle rushed over to hug him gently.

"Are you all right?" Lyle murmured in his ear.

"I will be." Eric wasn't all right yet, he had to admit he was still in shock.

"You let your Daddy take care of you. Don't try to be brave."

"You don't mind me staying longer?" He wasn't sure how they'd feel about it. He was a stranger after all. "I can't work for a while." He wasn't looking forward to that conversation with his publisher.

"I don't think Brad is going to let you out of his sight," Lyle assured him.

Eric waited for him to add to that, but Lyle stepped back and the other boys swarmed, Brad standing back to give him space. Even prickly Red hugged him. Aaron was the last, and he waited until Eric tugged him gently.

Eric spoke as Aaron opened his mouth. "Don't you dare apologize for something that's not your fault." He scowled at Aaron. "I mean it. You're not responsible for your mom's actions, and we all know she didn't mean to shoot me. She didn't really have a clue what she was doing."

"I don't know about that," Aaron muttered, but he relaxed a fraction, and when Jake came over, he relaxed into his Daddy's arms.

"I told you he wouldn't blame you," Jake chided, enfolding Aaron in his arms.

"You're not the only one with evil relatives," Matt agreed. "I mean, let's face it, my father was the prince of evil."

"My uncle," Jack added. "He was just nasty."

"My dad abandoned me," Vinny said. Then he wrinkled his brow. "I don't know if he's evil," he admitted.

"Our found family is the best though," Lyle said. "We got our fairytale ending."

Eric managed a smile. "You guys are the best."

He didn't want to talk about happy ever afters when he only had a happy for now.

Brad ran a hand down his back. "What do you want to do?"

"You should eat," Lyle said. "Just pot roast. It's just about ready. Then sleep. Otherwise you'll wake up in the middle of the night with a snarly belly."

They were all nodding at him and although Eric wasn't hungry, Lyle had a point.

"You can sit on my lap and rest until it's ready," Brad suggested.

Eric looked at him, uncertain if that was a good idea. He wasn't tiny like Vinny and felt he swamped Brad.

"I can manage," Brad assured him and sat at the table, tugging Eric onto his lip. It was strange but comfortable, and Brad's arms around him again was good, making him feel secure. The whole day had left him unbalanced. He buried his face in Brad's neck, loving the feel of his beard. Brad rubbed soothing circles on his back.

Conversation ebbed and flowed around him, but no one expected him to talk which was good, because he didn't feel he could hold a conversation just yet.

"Time for dinner," Brad rumbled in his ear.

Eric started and he realized he must have fallen asleep again. He seemed to do that a lot here. He sat up and yawned. "I'm sorry. I didn't mean to fall asleep."

"You had a busy day," PJ said as he helped himself to pot roast. "Getting shot does that to people."

Jack nudged his Daddy as Aaron cringed. "Let's try and forget about that for now."

"Sorry," PJ muttered to Aaron around a mouthful.

"We can't ignore it," Aaron admitted. "You know we're going to be dealing with the fallout from this too. Any court case will get extra publicity."

Eric looked up from the plate of pot roast, mashed potatoes, and vegetables Lyle had put in front of him. "Do you think this will go to trial?"

Aaron pursed his lips, then shook his head. "I don't think she's well enough to stand trial. But it's not my decision. Are you okay with that? She shot you after all."

Eric thought about it for a while. "She didn't mean to hit me. She didn't know what she was doing."

He wasn't sure he fully believed that, and from the look on Aaron's, Alec's, and Matt's faces, they definitely didn't, but he hated the idea of standing up in court.

Chatter died away as they ate and Eric focused on the meal in front of him. He was going to miss this food when he left. Lyle and Vinny cooked the best food ever. Eating wasn't easy on Brad's lap but his Daddy seemed determined not to let him go. He ate more than half of the food, then he sat back against Brad's chest and relaxed.

"Hey, how about we spend time in the playroom tomorrow when we're more relaxed," Jake suggested.

Eric nodded thankfully. He was too stressed to regress into his little right now. A thought had struck him and that needed all his adult Eric to handle. He tilted his head to look at Brad. "I need to call David Peterson today or at least leave him a message."

"Okay. Once we're done here, we'll go upstairs and you can call him."

Eric chewed on his bottom lip. He wasn't sure how his boss would take another delay. He knew they were excited by the poems and the illustrations so far to match them. But he was a freelance artist and this was Brad's debut book. Would his publisher wait for the time for his arm to heal or would they send out another artist? He wouldn't know until they had that conversation.

Chapter Nine

Brad

Brad led Eric up the stairs and herded him into his bedroom without the usual discussion of whether Eric wanted to go to his own room. He switched on the small lamp on the nightstand. Eric let out a long sigh and when Brad checked his expression, he realized Eric was relieved to be with him.

He cupped Eric's jaw and stared into his stormy eyes. "You never have to ask to be with me, sweet boy. Your place is in my arms."

"It's where I want to be," Eric admitted, "but I don't want to pressure you. I'm a nobody, an orphan kid who can't remember anything. You don't have to take care of me."

That had to be the shock after the day talking, because Brad wasn't sure how much clearer he could make it to Eric that the only place he wanted his boy was in his arms.

"You're my boy," he said, stroking Eric's cheek with his thumb. "You are and always will be my boy."

"You barely know me," Eric whispered.

"We were kissing within five minutes of meeting each other," Brad pointed out.

"I don't remember," Eric said wistfully.

"I'll remember enough for both of us," Brad assured him. "Now let's get that call over and done with."

"What if he says he's going to send a new artist or worse, cancel your book?"

Brad shrugged. "I don't want a new artist and if he cancels the book then so be it."

"But it's your dream."

Brad shook his head. "You're my dream, my sweet boy. The idea of a book is lovely, but the events of the past couple of years have made me realize the only things I care about are right here with me. You, my brothers, their boys, that daft mutt. What more could I need?"

Eric's eyes shone in the low light of the bedroom and Brad knew he was close to tears.

He wanted to make love to his boy now, but Eric still had to call the publisher. Brad should have made him do it downstairs. This was their private space.

"Call David," he ordered gently. "Put it on speaker."

He didn't have any right to hear the call and he wouldn't have argued if Eric had said no, but his boy just nodded.

He drew Eric over to the bed and they sat cuddled against the pillows while Eric waited for the call to connect.

"David Peterson."

Brad wished it had reached the voicemail.

"David, it's Eric."

"Eric, I was going to give you a call. Is the book nearly ready? What's happening with our reluctant poet?"

Eric grimaced at him. "You're on speaker with him."

"Evening, David," Brad said cheerfully.

"Oh...right...Bradley...how are you?"

Peterson wasn't pleased at being caught out. It was plain in his voice.

"David, I asked Eric to put you on speaker. There's been an issue and the illustrations will be delayed."

"What kind of issue?" Peterson said sharply. "We're running behind schedule, Bradley. You know that. We can't afford another delay."

"Eric was shot in the arm."

Silence.

Then, "I'm sorry? Did you say 'shot'?"

"Eric was shot in the arm by a crazed woman. It's a minor wound but he needs time to recover."

More silence. Eric flinched and Brad wrapped him up in his arms.

"David, I'll understand if you need to replace me."

"No. I want Eric to do my illustrations, no one else," Brad stated. "You've seen what he did. They're perfect."

"They are," Peterson agreed, almost reluctantly. "But someone else could replicate—"

"No," Brad said again. "It has to be Eric."

"Bradley—"

"For the love of God, call me Brad, like I've asked you a hundred times. Look, David, it's as simple as this. Eric is a Kingdom boy."

The long silences were starting to grate on his nerves. Eric was visibly upset now.

"He's what?"

"He's a Kingdom boy."

"How do you know? Eric, have you regained your memory?"

"No," Eric said.

"I met Eric just before his accident," Brad said. "He was

in the Kingdom Theme Park, the same as the other boys... my brothers' partners. We knew who he was as soon as he arrived."

"But that's wonderful. It'll be so good for the publicity."

Brad and Eric grimaced at each other. It was always about the bottom line, the mighty dollar.

"So you'll understand if Eric has time off to heal the wound, then he can finish up."

"I haven't got many more to do, David," Eric said, "and I'll send you the recent ones."

"Okay. Is Eric safe?" Finally, he showed some concern for his employee.

"The woman is in the custody of the sheriff. She needs medical help."

"We can't sue her?"

Eric muttered something under his breath that Brad didn't catch. "I don't think so. I just need a few days, David, then we'll be finished."

"We have to go now. Eric needs the rest," Brad said. "I'll call you when I have more information. Goodnight."

He disconnected the call on David's "Wait, I've got something—"

"Maybe he had something to tell me," Eric said.

"It can wait until tomorrow."

Brad had one thing in mind for his boy and it wasn't an endless conversation with David Petersen. He'd spoken to the man before and it was always an effort to get away from him.

"Time for you and me, my boy," Brad murmured.

Eric snorted and settled down in his arms.

Brad sighed and gave a rueful smile. Maybe not. The day had finally caught up with his boy. He contemplated just closing his eyes and joining Eric in sleep, but they'd be more comfortable undressed.

He moved Eric, who grumbled, but didn't wake up. Eric could stay there while he had a shower. He needed to wash away the strains of the day.

* * *

It took a long time for Brad to fully open his eyes. He just didn't want to be awake. He kissed the nape of Eric's neck, not sure if he was awake or not. No one had knocked on the door to get him up, so he guessed they'd made a decision to handle all the chores today. He was grateful and would return the favor another time. For now, he just wanted to take care of his boy.

Eric sighed and burrowed back into Brad's embrace. "What time is it?" he murmured.

"I don't know," Brad admitted. "Later than usual. It's light outside already."

"I'm sorry. Do you need to work?"

Brad tightened his hold. "I'm staying with you. My brothers can manage the farm."

"But—"

"Just let me take care of you. You can't work and you need to rest your arm. You can spend the day being my boy."

Eric sighed. "I'd like that."

"But first..." Brad slid his hand around to Eric's cock, loving the sudden squeak from his boy. "We need to catch up from last night."

"You want me to—"

"I want you to stay where you are while I make you come apart," Brad ordered.

"Yes, sir." Eric sighed happily.

"Daddy," Brad corrected.

"Yes, Daddy," Eric said obediently.

PJ was right about one thing. His boy did take orders very well. He wouldn't tell his brother that. He'd be unbearable.

Eric moaned and spread his legs, giving Brad more access.

"Good boy," Brad praised, loving the feel of silky skin over Eric's hardening cock.

"I love my Daddy Braddy."

No one had ever had a special name for Brad. He treasured it to his heart.

A sound trilled out, breaking Brad's concentration.

"That's my phone," Eric said apologetically.

Brad sighed and let go of his boy. Eric grabbed it from the nightstand and frowned as he squinted at the screen. "It's David. What does he want?"

Brad yawned, not happy at his cozy time with his boy being disturbed. "I don't know, my boy. Why don't you answer and find out. Then we can get back to our time together."

Eric grunted and pressed connect, then speaker. "Hi David, is everything all right?"

"Everything's fine. More than fine." His publisher's voice boomed out, almost too much in their private space. "I wanted to tell you this late night. I've got great news for you, Eric. A children's author saw your illustrations and he wants you to illustrate his books. As soon as you've finished with this book, you'll be flying to Florida for at least six months, maybe a year."

Eric

Eric wasn't sure where to start. They all knew about the job offer. He took a deep breath.

"I'm used to being second. I come after the author or the poet." His illustrations developed their world. He was comfortable with that.

They all nodded, and he gained a little confidence. These boys understood him.

"My Daddy makes the decisions."

But now Brad wanted him to take the lead, to make a decision which would affect or end their relationship, and Eric wasn't sure he could do that.

"You have to tell him," Lyle said, over the rim of his cup. "Brad's a kind man. He'll understand."

There was a chorus of agreement and nodding. Eric thought they all looked like nodding dogs.

Vinny flopped down on a beanbag and Rexy crawled on top of him for a snuggle. "We've got to stop giving him treats," Vinny grumbled.

"You say that to our Daddies," Aaron said pointedly.

It was true, the dog was starting to look portly around the middle, but trying to ban the brothers from sneaking Rexy treats was impossible.

"Get PJ to run him over the farm," Jack suggested. "He just needs more exercise. We've all hibernated over the winter."

This was also true. It had been a harsh winter after Christmas, and the family had spent the time together. Even Jake and Alec had declared they were working in their office at home rather than being cut off from the family when the mountain road closed. Their boys had confided to Eric that they were glad of the time together.

But, back to Eric's current predicament.

"I don't know what to do. I want to say no, but this job is everything I wanted."

"The children's author wants you to illustrate all his books?" Red asked. He was snuggled against Matt under a blanket Aaron had knitted. Aaron was into making things, not always with great success. But the blanket was warm and colorful, and they could forgive a few holes.

"Yes."

"And there's like, a hundred of them?"

"Yes."

"In Florida?"

Eric nodded again.

"And the author wants you to fly to Florida and work on them there."

Eric heard the wistful note in Red's voice. Florida was Red's home, not here on the mountain, and he missed it, no matter how hard he tried to hide it.

"He does," Eric agreed. "It's a great opportunity, but..."

"But you'd be away from your Daddy for months," Lyle said softly.

"He could go with you," Matt suggested.

Eric huffed, scowling into his hot chocolate. "The author's agent and publisher doesn't think it's a good idea for the public to know about Brad, or the family."

The room went quiet and he looked to see everyone watching him. "What?" Then, "Oh, yeah, they really did say that."

Vinny scowled at him. "And you didn't tell them to—"

Lyle slapped a hand over his mouth. "What Vinny was trying to say was—"

Eric gave a wry grin as he interrupted. "I know what he

was trying to say and I should have told them to, but I was so shocked, you know?"

"One minute they were offering you the job of your dreams and the next they were telling you that you'd have to hide who you were?" Matt suggested.

"Yeah, and I hated that." Eric frowned, scowling at his cup again. "I love my Daddy. I don't want to hide him."

Silence again.

He looked up to see six, no seven, Rexy woke up to stare at him, pairs of eyes on him. "What now?"

"I think you've just answered your own question," Red said.

Eric sighed. "It's not as easy as that."

"Why not?" Vinny said. "You just say no."

"One, if I turn this down they might not give me another opportunity and two, Brad is determined that I should take the job."

"Brad wants you to go?" Aaron asked doubtfully.

"No, he hates the idea. But he doesn't want to stand in my way."

"You know, Daddies can be real stupid sometimes," Vinny confided. "We've nearly all had this conversation with our Daddies."

"You have?"

"Oh yeah," Red agreed. "Harry kept talking about birds and flying."

"Damien hid in a barn for weeks," Vinny added.

Aaron nodded. "Jake took me down to the motel so I could get the bus out of town."

"PJ was a bit distracted with everyone being away," Jack admitted.

"And I was the one running away," Matt murmured.

Aaron hugged Matt against him. "The point is, none of

us want to be away from our Daddies, but this is a decision you'll have to make, not him. He's giving you the freedom to do that."

"I hate it," Eric said fiercely. "I want him to make that decision for me."

"But he won't," Lyle, who'd mainly kept quiet, said. "Because our Daddies aren't like that. They want us to be happy and if that means letting us go, they would. All of us."

"Like Gruff would let you out of his sight," Matt scoffed.

Eric ached at Lyle's sweet grin. He wanted that too.

Then Red put his arm around Eric's shoulders. "Don't listen to us, little brother. We're all different. You tell Brad what you want and that's for him to make the decision for you."

"Do you think he will?" Eric asked in a small voice.

"I think he'll move heaven and earth to make you happy, so you show him that's what you want."

Eric nodded against Red's shoulder. It was always a shock when prickly Red showed affection, but his advice was good. He needed to talk to his Daddy.

* * *

"Baby boy?"

Eric looked over at Brad's sleepy voice in the darkness.

"Why are you out of bed?"

"I couldn't sleep," Eric admitted. "I didn't want to disturb you."

"You should wake me if you can't sleep. That's what I'm here for."

Brad rolled out of bed and came over to the window.

113

Eric sighed in pleasure as Brad stood behind him, wrapped his arms around his body and rested his cheek on Eric's head.

"You feel so warm." Eric almost purred at the pleasure.

"You're cold," Brad scolded.

"I'm sorry, Daddy. I just needed to think. My mind wouldn't switch off."

"Do you want to talk about it?"

Eric sighed. "No, but we have to."

He felt tension flood Brad's muscles.

"It's about the job opportunity?" Brad asked.

"Yes."

"You should take it."

"You hate the idea," Eric said. "You can't deny it."

Brad sighed, his breath ruffling Eric's hair. "I do hate it, but I'd never stand in your way."

"I want you to," Eric said fiercely. "I want you to say no and tie me to the bed. Say that you hate the idea of me leaving the mountain and I'm here forever."

Brad turned Eric around to face him. Eric tried to look away but Brad caught his chin and forced Eric to look into his eyes, the blue washed out in the moonlight.

"And what happens when you suddenly remember the opportunity you lost because of me?"

"I turned it down because my love for you is more important than staying away for half a year with an author who hates the idea of me and you."

"It might not be the author," Brad said.

Eric waved his hand. "I don't care. I love you."

"And I love you too. Wait, did you say you'd turned the job down?"

"I sent them an email before I went to bed. I apologized but said I wasn't prepared to spend half a year away from the best thing that ever happened to me and if they couldn't accommodate that, I wasn't the right person for the job. Then I shut the laptop and walked away."

"Oh baby."

Brad gathered Eric against his fur. Eric squeezed his eyes shut and let the few tears be soaked up by Brad's chest hair. For all he said, turning down the job of his dreams hurt like hell, but he'd do it for them. Because his Daddy was more important than anything else.

Brad picked up Eric's hand and pressed a kiss into his palm. "Thank you, my boy. You don't know how much this means to me." Further tears spilled onto Eric's cheeks and Brad wiped them away with his thumb. "Let's go back to bed."

Eric let Brad draw him away from the window and into their bed, still warm from Brad's body.

Brad drew him into his arms. "We'll talk about this again in the morning, but for now you go to sleep and know you are the only boy of my heart."

Eric closed his eyes. That's all he really needed. Anything else was the cherry on top.

Epilogue

One year later

Brad

"He's hiding again," PJ grumbled.

Brad rolled his eyes. He was kind of hiding, but not in his barn. He was hiding outside the kitchen door, waiting for his cue to come in.

"He's outside," Vinny said. "Look at Rexy."

"Brad?"

Brad opened the door as Eric laughed out his name. "You boys know how to ruin a surprise," he grumbled.

"I told you, Rexy is a snitch," Matt said, leaning against Alec as he usually did.

"He's the best dog in the world," Damien cooed, scratching the black mutt under his chin. The dog closed his eyes and one back leg went into overdrive.

Gruff squinted at Brad. "It's not Christmas yet. Who are the gifts for?"

"For you, one per couple."

Brad went around the table, handing one to each of his brothers. They all looked up at him. "Go on, open it."

He slumped in the seat next to Eric and waited for his brothers to open their present.

"It's your poetry book," Gruff said.

PJ whooped. "Big brother is finally in print!"

"Just open it," Eric suggested, his tone soft.

"I've read his poetry and I don't understand a word," Harry admitted.

But they all opened their books, the Daddies peering over their boys' shoulders, and the table went silent.

"Oh my God," Lyle managed. He looked up, his expression awed. "This is me under the tree." He pointed to a pen and ink illustration under the first poem.

PJ barked out a laugh. "And this is me knocking Jack unconscious."

"This is how we met our boys," Damien murmured. "This is me holding your hand, Vinny."

Vinny sobbed and flung himself into Damien's arms.

"The reason you didn't understand the poetry was because you thought it was about the explosions," Eric explained, "when it was about something else entirely."

"Well, I have a lot of poems about blowing shit up," Brad admitted and dug in his pocket for a dollar. "But this book is about my family, my brothers, and their boys, my little brothers."

Alec turned to Eric. "You did all the illustrations?"

Eric's smile was sweet. "If you remember, I asked all of you how you remembered your first meeting."

The table went silent again as they leafed through the book.

"Oh."

Everyone turned to Damien who stared at Brad, tears rolling down his cheeks. "You wrote about Mom and Dad."

"I had to," Brad said simply. "They are why we're here."

Then he yelped as his six brothers converged on him, hugging him senseless, then they hugged Eric too for the illustrations which brought their relationships to life. Then it was the boys' turn.

"Thank you," Brad heard Vinny whisper to Eric. "You made my Daddy so handsome."

"He is handsome." Eric was confused.

Vinny beamed at him, his smile lighting up the kitchen. "I know he is."

Eric furrowed his brow. "I don't understand. All our Daddies are handsome."

And Damien looked away for a moment. Brad knew he was choked up. His big brother would never change.

He got up and gave Damien a bear hug. "You did good, big brother," he whispered.

Damien hung onto him, his shoulders shaking, and Brad just held him, knowing his brother didn't get nearly enough recognition for the way he'd kept the family together since their parents died. His younger brothers might not see it, but he was the next in line, and he'd seen Damien become the patriarch and hold the family in his arms.

Then Vinny was there and Brad guided Damien into Vinny's arms.

"You know they love you," he heard Vinny whisper in Damien's ear. "You only have to look at the book now to see it."

He slumped down next to Eric, and watched his brothers as they read through the book. He knew not all of them would understand his poetry, but they would know it came from his love for them.

Eric laced his fingers with Brad's. "Okay?" he murmured.

"Relieved," Brad admitted, his voice low so that only Eric could hear. "I think they like your drawings the most."

"Maybe," Eric agreed, "but they'll read the words and then they'll understand."

"Hey, Eric."

Eric looked over at Harry. "Yeah?"

"I thought you didn't remember the kissing by the woodshed."

"I don't." Eric blushed. "But you guys told me about it enough."

Brad stared at the illustration of them kissing. Yeah, it was pretty much like that in his memory.

"I can't believe your book is finally out," Lyle said.

"At least I sold six copies," Brad said, "even if it was to me."

Eric squinted at him. "Six?"

"Yeah, I bought six copies on Amazon and a couple more for friends." Brad watched Eric chew on his bottom lip. "What's wrong? Am I not allowed to do that? Is that like insider trading or something?"

Eric burst out laughing. "Oh, my Daddy, you have no idea, do you?"

"No idea about what?" Brad was genuinely confused, but the 'my Daddy' made him warm all over.

"You've sold more than six copies."

Brad brightened. "That's good. It would be good if Petersen Press could make their money back eventually."

At Eric's choking noise, Brad furrowed his brow. "Am I missing something?"

"You're going to have to tell him," Lyle said. "Is it time?"

"It's time," Eric said.

Red and Jack scurried out of the kitchen.

Brad had a sudden realization something was going on and he was involved. He looked around the table. His brothers looked as bewildered as him.

Jack poked his head around the door and Lyle nodded.

Balloons. Lots of balloons. Which filled the kitchen. But six boys including Eric stood in line.

"No, we need to move," Vinny said, giving the orders as usual. "Aaron, you need to come next to me."

They shuffled, reshuffled, then beamed at him.

He read the message.

BRADLEY BRENNER NEW YORK TIMES BESTSELLER

What?

"Fuck."

Seven brothers swore in unison.

"You're joking." Brad was convinced he was going to pass out.

Eric dropped his balloon and rushed over to hold his hands. "I'm not. You're number six in the bestseller list. You've sold thousands. David Petersen is over the moon. His assistant said he nearly choked on a blueberry muffin. He's never had a New York Times bestseller."

"But it's just a poetry book," Brad said faintly.

"About seven brothers on the side of a mountain who saved one boy, and he changed the world." Eric dug under the table and handed him a clipping from a paper. "This is the New York Times. That's from the review."

Brad swallowed hard and leaned forward to read it, then leaned back. "No, I don't want to read it in case they hated it."

Harry whisked it away from him and scanned it.

"You're safe, big brother. They loved it and gave it a five-star review. You can read it."

Brad swallowed again. Even now his brothers took care of him.

"I think we need timeout and cake," Lyle suggested and produced a giant red velvet cake iced in...

"Wait!" Brad leaned forward. "Is that one of your sketches?"

Eric grinned. "That's you blowing up the barn."

"Again," Gruff said.

Brad grinned sheepishly.

"My brother's a celebrity," PJ said. He turned to Jack. "I'm sorry. I can't be a celebrity." He actually looked worried.

Jack leaned up and kissed PJ's cheek. "I like you just as you are."

Brad grinned as his huge muscled mountain of a brother melted against his boy.

"Cake!" Gruff insisted.

"Wait!" Eric raised his voice and they all turned to him in surprise. He blushed. "I'm sorry, there's just one more thing I wanted to show you."

He looked at Brad who had been waiting for this and slipped out of the room.

"It's not another doggy, is it?" Vinny asked, looking worried.

Brad came back with a large frame as Eric spoke. "Rexy is the dog of the house," he assured him.

Eric took a deep breath. "This is one picture I wasn't prepared to show the world. It's for us, our family."

Brad turned it around and there were gasps from everyone. It was all the Daddies and all the boys in the playroom, not a sketch this time but a painting he'd spent weeks on.

"It's going to go up in our playroom," Brad said.

Aaron had a hand over his mouth. "I'm Anna."

"Is that all right?" Eric asked, worried he'd upset Aaron. He'd drawn her sitting on her Daddy's lap as he talked to Harry.

"More than okay," he said, his voice shaky.

Jake hauled him close against his chest and Eric heard the whispered, "My pretty girl."

Lyle and Jack played with trains. Matt leaned against Alec, he could have been dozing. Vinny held his Daddy's hand as he watched them play. Red sat with Eric, they seemed to be deep in conversation. PJ was eating as normal as he talked to Gruff and Brad.

Brad held his arms out to Eric. "You're amazing," he whispered in his boy's ear. He looked over his boy's head to Damien who for once wasn't crying. The patriarch of the family just looked proud. And so he should.

Eric buried his face into the crook of Brad's neck. "I'm never going to remember our first meeting even with the illustration."

"I know. But it doesn't matter. The only thing that matters is you and me. Besides," Brad gave a wicked grin, "we can always reenact our first meeting."

"He had his tongue down your throat within five minutes," Alec assured Eric. "We all saw it."

The brothers hummed their agreement.

Eric knew it, but it didn't stop him going bright red.

"Leave my boy alone," Brad ordered. "Only I'm responsible for making him blush."

"It's just you and me for the cake," Gruff said to Lyle. "We could take it up to the bedroom. We could have tub time." He waggled his eyebrows at Lyle.

With Brad and Eric moved out into their own cabin, it

was just Lyle and Gruff in the house. But the brothers still claimed tub privileges.

There was talk of filling the house with boys who needed help from the Kingdom theme parks, but Gruff had put his foot down and said Lyle needed time out for a while just to be his boy.

PJ claimed the cake and it got very noisy around the table.

By the end of the night, Brad was almost relieved to be walking back to their cabin with Eric, holding hands as usual. He loved his family and the celebration had been wonderful, but he needed time to decompress.

"Are you disappointed in me?" he asked suddenly.

Eric glanced up at him. "Why would I be disappointed?"

"Because I don't really want to be a celebrity."

He was surprised by Eric's low chuckle. "I told them you'd hate the idea of publicity."

"I'm a farmer."

Eric leaned against him and Brad slung an arm around his shoulder. "No, you're not. You're a poet, a farmer, and a chemist, a barber, a shoulder for your brothers. But most of all, you're my Daddy. Nothing else matters."

"You've ended up back on the mountain."

"I know," Eric agreed, "and that's kind of okay too. Um...David Petersen offered me another job. With even more books than the job I turned down."

"Oh?" Brad's voice reeked with tension.

Eric beamed at him. "I can work here. The author is local and said he'd like to visit occasionally, but otherwise we can work online. He's a bit of a recluse."

"That's wonderful." Brad swept him into a hug. "We'll build you a studio."

"That would be amazing, Daddy. Don't forget you promised to pose for me."

"How would you like me?"

Eric gave him an arch look. "Do I really need to answer that?"

Brad couldn't hide his blush and Eric outright giggled. He guessed it was a stupid question.

"My naughty boy will get a spanking."

Eric shivered. "Yes, please, Daddy."

Brad grinned. He would enjoy that as much as Eric.

"So we all stay on the mountain," Eric said.

"Seven boys for seven lonely brothers." Brad still had to get his head around that sometimes.

"Seven Daddies for seven lost boys," Eric amended.

Brad cupped Eric's jaw, tilted his head bathing his face in the silver starlight, and brushed Eric's lips. "But only one is the boy for me."

THE END

Thank you for reading Bear in Boots. We may have reached the end of Bearytales, but have you read the series that preceded my mountain men? Want to know how my series interlink?

LYON ROAD VETS

(From Stormin' Norman onward, although Jesse is introduced in Hazel Takes Over) - Jesse Waldron and Dan Miller

ANGEL SECURITIES

Crossover characters - Jesse Waldron, Dan Miller, Peter Mitchell, Evan Wells plus Lyon Road Vets characters

BIKER DADDY BODYGUARDS

Crossover characters - Josh Cooper, Dominic Cook from CDR

DARKER DADDY BODYGUARDS

Crossover characters - Josh Cooper, Dominic Cook, Quinn Ryder, Louis Romano

BEARYTALES SERIES

Crossover characters - Josh Cooper, Quinn Ryder

OTHER BOOKS

Island Doctor - Peter Mitchell and Evan Wells from Lyon Road Vets

A Cock in the Window - Owens family side characters from the Isle series

You can find all of them on my website.

www.suebrownstories.com

About the Author

Cranky middle-aged author with an addiction for coffee, and a passion for romancing two guys. She loves her dog, she loves her kids, and she loves coffee; in which order very much depends on the time of day.

Come over and talk to Sue at:

Newsletter: http://bit.ly/SueBrownNews
Bookbub: https://www.bookbub.com/profile/sue-brown
TikTok: https://www.tiktok.com/@suebrownstories
Patreon: https://www.patreon.com/suebrownstories
Her website: http://www.suebrownstories.com/
Author group – Facebook: https://www.facebook.com/groups/suebrownstories/
Facebook: https://www.facebook.com/SueBrownsStories/
Email: sue@suebrownstories.com

Printed in Great Britain
by Amazon

43267443R00078